DRAGONSONG

DRAGONSONG

MICHAEL FORESTER

Matador
9 Priory Business Park,
Wistow Road, Kibworth Beauchamp,
Leicestershire. LE8 0RX
Tel: 0116 279 2299
Email: books@troubador.co.uk
Web: www.troubador.co.uk/matador
Twitter: @matadorbooks

ISBN 978 1785891 274

British Library Cataloguing in Publication Data.
A catalogue record for this book is available from the British Library.

Printed and bound in the UK by TJ International, Padstow, Cornwall
Typeset in 11pt Garamond by Troubador Publishing Ltd, Leicester, UK

Matador is an imprint of Troubador Publishing Ltd

This is for the Seer,
who has finally come to believe he has the power of sight.

It is for the Lady Attie,
who very probably saved the Seer's sanity.

It is for Harmony,
with the fervent wish that one day she will recognise her capacity for love.

But most of all, it is for the Lords of Fire and Ice,
who maybe, maybe, now will sleep.

CONTENTS

BOOK THE FIRST

LADY ATTIE OF THE LAKE

PROLOGUE

I

Last night I lay upon my cot
and slumber sweetly to me came.
Thus I was still and toss-ed not
and sleep did not eschew my frame.
Then came wing-ed Mercury unto me.
He from his scabbard drew his sword
and steel upon my eyelids lay
and quoth he, "Rise, speak not a word
and flee from here before the day
for there is much that I must show to thee."

II

Thou art a scribe and thou must write
what I shall show unto thine eyes
employing always second sight
that those that read will realise
that thou hast seen and truly speak no guile.
Thus rose we to the astral plane
and travelled far o'er land and sea
and to a place we surely came
when map-ed out was destiny
and rested we, and spoke and mused awhile.

1
THE BIRTH OF THE LADY

III

Then back to Gaia did descend,
mine eyes did spy whence we would go
and saw at once our journey's end –
a land called Freedom far below
there to behold a tale of epic grace.
The land was ruled by judges, three.
Each bore their name upon their breast
Faith, Love and True Equality.
This was enough – for all the rest
would follow sweetly from these in their place.

IV

He led me to a wooded lake;
to cabin rude with earthen floor –
a woman working – she did make
for husband, victuals (and some more
lest strangers sought to sojourn in her gate).
Then almost if at her behest,
a beggar came in garments torn
who sought refreshment – food and rest
and by her fire himself to warm.
Then thought she first, Nay, for the hour is late.

V

But check-ed she her foremost thought
and to the beggar did afford
the food and rest that he had oought
thus ceased he journeying abroad
and at the woman's cabin he did wait.
Then quoth he to her, speaking low,
"Dear Madam, hast thou daughter, son?"
And she replied, "I answer no.
My heart it bleeds that I have none...
and now for cause of age it is too late."

VI

"Then know this, Madam, speak I right.
When to thy bed thy husband comes,
thou shalt conceive this very night
and thus thy misery be undone."
And as he spoke he touched her on her womb.
Then dropp-ed she her eyes to earth
in fear lest he did speak a lie.
She knew that hope to have great worth
but if untrue then she would die
and make her husband place her in her tomb.

VII

But when she raised her eyes again
no beggar there did she behold –
only the lake in softest rain
was shadowed, but in burning gold
the sun, she did descend upon the earth.
And thus the two did rainbow make,
and colour merged to coloured hue.
And then she did this promise make
(for knew the beggar had spoke true)
"My child shall be to Gaia of great worth!"

VIII

Then, as the months did pass away
she felt the life inside her grow
and knew with every passing day
(with certainty she came to know)
upon the birth the beggar would return.
As Autumn unto Winter turned
and ice upon the lake was formed
her heart, expectant for March, yearned
and when the first and twentieth dawned
she knew the babe for life within her turned.

IX

Thus, babe within her now full-formed
could not restrain impending cry –
sprang forth in ecstasy adorned
Life! Life! Take breath or I shall die!
A girl child, beauteous, grey-blue-eyed and true.
Exhausted now upon the bed
the mother lay with babe in arms
then knock at door brought her no dread
she knew the beggar came – no harm
to bring but prophecy would come anew.

X

The beggar held the babe to heart
and spoke to her in prophecy
and for her life set her apart
and named her there as Natalie
"For all thy days shalt thou the truth uphold.
'Tis written in thy stars, fair child
that thou shalt be a warrior true
defending weak and meek and mild
and keeping justice in thy view
make trial by combat for the just less bold."

XI

Then the o'er the babe he passed his hands
invisibly he mark-ed her
that those that came from magic lands
to spirit strong would full defer
and leave her grow in peace and strength and grace.
Then to the mother gave her back
and promising he would resort
each birthday to the little shack
with gift that would the child support
as she her future did begin to trace.

II
THE SPELL AND THE GIFTS

XII

The child was beauteous; fair of face.
Her fame throughout the land did grow
and all that knew her saw her grace
and wanted Natalie to know
and some discerned that magic had been done.
Then as she grew by lakeside shore
she found her feet and found her voice
she ran and played and chattered more
but could not speak her name of choice
thus 'Natalie' did 'Attie' soon become.

XIII

The child's great worth was soon made known
to Oberon of Elfindom.
Within his Pool of Sight was shown
The mighty warrior she'd become
And thus King Oberon a plan devised,
to take the child as if his own
and in her place would leave instead
an elfin girl in Attie's home
and to her mother cause great dread
to spread confusion, misery and lies.

XIV

At night he did to lakeside steal
with elfin soldiers, swords in hand
and would unto the child reveal
his purpose dark within the land
thus to steal Attie from her cabin home.
But curses! As he touched the bed
it burned with flame and fire of grace
preventing him from purpose dread
to leave the elf child in her place
and warned was he to leave her well alone.

XV

And then within him anger burned!
His face contorted in a rage
and spake he, as from her he turned
for nought that anger would assuage,
"Two blessings and a curse I leave at last.
The first is this: thou shalt be wise.
The second this: thou shalt speak true.
But if thou stay in human guise
the third I now speak unto you:
that all thy days in solitude shall pass."

XVI

And with a roar that shook the land
and woke the trees from slumber long,
the elfin child he took by hand.
So in a moment they were gone –
and ne'er again would darken lakeside shore.
The child slept on and in her dreams
possessed of love and purity
she wandered lake and forest streams
and dreamt of what she soon would be
champion of grace and truth for evermore.

XVII

So Attie grew and on each year,
her birth was marked by visits new
from beggar, bearing gifts to her
and each her coming life reviewed
as if to set her heart upon the way.
One year a sword (of truth) he gave
the next a breastplate (righteousness)
and then a shield (of faith), be brave!
And thou thy spirit shall possess
to set thy heart on tasks of coming day.

XVIII

As Attie grew the fairy's proof
upon her evidenced itself.
For though she gained in wisdom, truth
and perfect beauty, grace and health
the love of men her heart could not include.
She lived alone by lake and tree
And in the cabin spent her days.
Herself she kept for company
Recluse she was, in all her ways.
Thus, all her days were spent in solitude.

XIX

For men would look upon her face
and in her beauty they would see
a woman gainly, full of grace
but one that spoke soliloquy,
for dialogue was not the way she trod.
Yet Attie hungered for a mate
of soul and heart and body too
a man to come unto her gate
and love her ever, honest true.
Yet none did come and place foot on her sod.

III
THE CHAMPION

XX

Now when she was full thirty year
and all those days had passed alone
the beggar came again to her
and told her time was to leave home.
And thence unto the judges she must go.
"Dear Attie," spake the beggar last.
"'Tis time for thee to part from me.
The years of preparation past
have readied thee for destiny.
Thou must now champion righteousness alone."

XXI

So Attie gathered all her garb
and took what little she possessed
closed cabin door (in truth 'twas hard)
– she headed north at his behest
then to show herself to Judges three.
And thus she journeyed far afield
she travelled both by day and night
with breastplate, sword and carrying shield
until the courthouse was in sight
Thus, there at last to meet her destiny.

XXII

Her fame had gone before her there
the Judges knew of her repute.
They welcomed Lady Attie fair
as one who dealt in purest truth
and thus they bid her champion weaker sorts.
The custom ruled in Freedom then
that trial by combat was their way
and men sought champions in strong men
who battled true through night and day
till truth did vanquish error in the heart.

XXIII

So thus for four and ten years long
did Attie carve her destiny
and vanquish error; falsehood; wrong;
and all the while was solitary
(though many suitors did her heart pursue).
And thus it was at forty four –
the fairy's curse still on her heart –
though beauteous, sweet and full demure
and though she sought a better part,
accepted Attie, love would not be true.

XXIV

Thus came the day that she did know,
despite the cause she championed true,
the time had come for her to go
and seek a destiny anew.
Thus, back unto the cabin Attie came.
And there she dwelt until the fall
did come and find her still bereft.
She cried to heaven "Is this all
that I shall know until cold death
doth take me, wrench me from this mortal frame?"

XXV

But heav'n was silent all that night
and snows of winter soon began –
turned lake to ice and forest white
and still she dwelt without a man
to comfort, hold her, love her through the night.
Thus, Attie's heart was fit to break
"What good is beauty?" would she cry
"If I cannot a lover take
and be beloved before I die?"
Thus Attie sought to set the heavens alight.

IV

THE COMING OF THE SEER

XXVI

She took to wandering forest old,
with heavy heart and face turned down;
wrapped up in fur to keep from cold
did Lady Attie of renown
pass all her lonely days in solitude.
"Frail men see beauty," she did muse
"and not the heart that in me dwells
thus lust for love they do confuse
betwixt the two they cannot tell.
And thus I am deprived of plenitude."

XXVII

One winter's day as she did walk
she happened on a hidden dell.
And there to her surprise, heard talk
in accent strange – she could not tell
where such a voice could thus originate.
The owner of the voice did speak
soliloquy unto the trees
he talked as if his heart would break
and kneel-ed he upon his knees
as pain and passion did he thus exude:

XXVIII

"I am a Seer of Albion
Arthurian court, it is my home.
Three years it is I have been gone
to travel o'er this land alone.
For she I seek is now lost from mine eyes.
I used to see, but now, twice blind,
with love for she who is my life
mine eyes are closed and sight of mind
did me desert – I sought a wife
And I have given all to seek this prize."

XXIX

The Seer wept upon his knees
for love long lost and left behind.
And Attie, curious to see
approached the stranger, deep of mind
whose pain did touch her deep within her heart.
Quoth she unto the Seer's face,
"Good sir, pray tell what troubles thee?
And whence com'st thou upon this place
for it is plain that I can see
a man of Freedom thou art surely not."

XXX

The Seer startled at her voice –
placed hands in front him to protect
said, "Madam, think thou this my choice
to be left blind, of love bereft?
Nay, surely thou canst see what I do seek?"
Spake Attie, "Yea, 'tis written clear
upon thy face and hands and heart
and I must tell thee, foreign Seer,
dwells no one here about these parts
that could be she whom you do say you seek."

XXXI

"But for love's sake I shall help thee
discern where she doth now abide
and if in Freedom she shall be
then I shall bring her to thy side.
Then thou with she shall once more be conjoined."
The Seer lifted up his head
and howled to sun and moon and sky,
"I cannot tell and thus do dread
for I have lost sight from my eyes
and deeper yet the sight within my mind."

XXXII

"There was a time in days long past
when faraway in Albion
I would have sought her soul at last
by travel on the astral plane
but now, from blindness there I cannot go.
But thou hast strength and art right whole
and thus could travel in my stead
there to seek her beauteous soul
and tell her of my foremost dread –
that she is there, but I am here below."

XXXIII

Thought Attie long and silently
and pondered on this arduous task.
Then saw the Seer on his knees
and knew that it would come to pass.
She could not leave one torn by such great need.
And thought she thus, but spake it not,
If he be blind and cannot see
(a man of substance here is caught)
by beauty he will not judge me
but know me only for my heart and deeds.

XXXIV

And could I love one such as this
who looks on heart and not on face?
If he were free I'd plant a kiss
and as his lover take my place.
Then all my days of solitude would pass.
A man of insight would I take
(and call him husband in my heart)
unto my cabin by the lake.
We happy two would never part!
My weary soul would find its rest at last.

XXXV

Alas though, it can never be.
This Seer loves another's heart.
Beaut'ous and worthy, strong is she
and from her he will never part –
but love her all their days together true.
And I am sworn to serve such love.
Thus rise I, at this man's behest
and I shall search the heav'ns above.
The Seer shall his love possess
and I shall meet my destiny anew.

XXXVI

Thus Attie to the Seer spoke
and said, "Good sir, tell me thy name
and name thy love, thy source of hope
I seek her now on astral plane
and when I find, shall bring her unto thee."
"Dear madam, I can tell no lie
my name is from my memory fled
but thou art love personified
and in thee do I find no dread.
For spek'st thou truly, softly unto me."

XXXVII

"My name... It meaneth 'like the Lord'.
My lover's name is Harmony
and music makes she by her words
her soul sings sweetly unto me.
And thus I am by love so deep possessed.
If thou canst find her on the plane
(and I will know it when you do)
just speak then unto her the same
and she will find me then anew.
Thus both our hearts shall once again find rest."

XXXVIII

"Then, if my name shall speak-ed be
(my lover true must say it first)
then I shall from dark spells be free
my eyes shall see the light at last
and second sight shall I possess anew."
"Then sir, to make thy spirit free
I shall now rise to astral plane
and seek her out, thy Harmony.
I'll bid her boldly speak thy name
and thou once more shall free-ed be full true."

XXXIX

And with that Attie drew her sword
and thrice did turn upon the ground.
The winds did rush, the heavens roared
and Christendom shook at the sound.
Then Attie to the astral plane was gone.
The forest then was silent, cold
with sunlight weak upon the lake
and in the mountains, aeons old,
the bears did long of sleep partake.
The Seer stood and mused in silence long.

V

HARMONY DISCOVERED

XL

Thus, Attic travelled astral plane.
Three days, three nights she travelled on
and food and water did disdain.
She would not eat till task was done
and she had made the blinded one to see.
A country strange did she behold
the mountains black, the valleys green
of auras coloured deepest gold
the like of which she had not seen
and still she sought the Seer's Harmony.

XLI

Now, every spirit she passed there
to each she put the question same:
"Please, hast thou seen a woman fair
Sweet Harmony, it be her name?"
But each one swiftly from her turned their face.
"In fear," she said unto herself.
"The reason why I cannot see
I only ask each one for help
in finding sweetest Harmony.
Confusion surely reigneth in this place!"

XLII

And on the fourth day she did spy
a darkest place at Eventide
as Attie sought a place to lie
saw darker cave on mountainside
and from inside a burning fire did flame.
Not being one to shirk in fear
she drew not back at sight of smoke
but placed herself to cave, right near
and thus unto the dragon spoke
with summoned courage, "Foul one, speak thy name."

XLIII

Then, from the cave came strangest sound.
It was no screeching as she'd thought
but sweetest voice as if she found
a maiden fair, of softer sort.
And spake the voice, "Now, who seeks Harmony?"
Then all at once she saw the truth!
The Seer, blinded by a spell,
had thought a maiden, fair, of youth
did hold his heart – he could not tell
the foul and desperate thing that she might be.

XLIV

The anger welled in Attie's frame.
For Seer, sweet was thus beguiled
and fear, though present, was disdained
for she would champion Seer mild
and unto trial by combat take the worm.
"Thou dragon foul – come forth to me
there is a service thou shalt give.
If thou, compliant now will be
perchance I might just let thee live.
Step forth! For there is something I must learn."

XLV

Then from the cave came shuffling sound
and fiery breath it did exude
and spittle fell upon the ground
and thus, foul form it did protrude
from cave mouth seven serpents' heads did come.
The dragon roared and shook the plane
and fire broke forth from serpent's cave.
Its human voice it did disdain:
"What dost thou seek, frail human, brave?
Speak quickly, then thy death shall surely come."

XLVI

"For clearly, when thy learning's done
and I have spoke at thy behest
thou shalt not live to see the dawn
thy death shall come from foolishness.
So tell me, what thou dost now seek of me?"
Then Attie drew her sword and cried,
"The Seer of Albion came to me
(to one I love thou hast long lied)
and bid me find his Harmony.
His name, oh foul one, I require of thee."

XLVII

"For thou hast put him to the spell
and taken from him both his sights.
Thou even now his name shall tell
and thy great wrong shall put aright
before I plunge my sword upon my word."
The dragon pondered for while
and through its evil memory sought.
It then replied with dragonish smile,
"Now I remember – Arthur's court...
the Seer, Michael, who is like the Lord."

XLVIII

And at that name the heavens shook
and shaft of light to earth descend
upon the Seer by the brook
and thus the spell was at an end
and Michael spoke his name and saw anew.
With second sight now full restored
he rose up high to astral plane
and needing not to speak a word
thus, unto Attie's side he came
and then at last beheld the dragon's spew.

XLIX

Spake dragon soft in human voice,
"Dear Michael, love'st thou Harmony?
Speak quickly now and make thy choice –
will it be Attie or be me?
And if it be me I will love thee true.
What need have we of human form
if dwell we here on astral plane?
With love I shall thee now adorn
and we shall lovers be again
then I shall warm thy heart again once more."

L

The Seer, weakened by the spell
exhausted, fell upon the ground.
"Be gone, thou serpent – get to Hell
where demons like thee do abound
for Attie now my soul has freed from thee."
And with that, fainted right away
that Attie feared him to be dead.
So with the light of coming day
did call his name and speak her dread,
"Dear Michael! Live! And now my lover be."

LI

And with that to the serpent turned
who smiled at her its serpent's sneer
"Ahhhhh… be he dead, for whom thou yearn?
Then thou should now be full of fear
to face sweet Harmony here all alone.
Now I shall kiss thee for my part
with seven mouths and seven tongues.
Let serpent venom fill thy heart
and thou shalt know thy pain begun
and maybe thus for foolishness atone."

LII

But Attie filled with rage, not fear
(her love she thinks dead on the soil)
did rise with sword and purpose clear
to make the serpent burn in hell
and from it severed heads, one, two and three.
The serpent shrieked in pain and fear
and to its cave it did withdraw
But Attie gave no mercy – clear
in her own heart in what she saw.
The dragon – full destroy-ed it must be.

LIII

Thus Attie pressed her vantage home
and with strokes four did slay it dead
such that it did with life atone
and with its blood and seven heads
for evil wrought in court of Albion.
Th' Arthurian Seer lay yet still
as Attie now, her tears did flow.
her love was lost, and thus her will
to live was sapped, and she would go
unto her love in death, to heaven he'd gone.

LIV

Whilst Attie chose twixt life and grave,
to live, or to her lover go,
came wing-ed Mercury to me
and said, "Scribe – thou dost fully know
that which is needful to permit a tale
of truth and love to be set down.
So, take thy pen and write it so.
For now our time here, it is done
and thence to earth we must now go.
To set thy quill a-writing, do not fail!"

LV

And thus it is, I tell no lie
and set forth truth before thy face
did Attie live – did Michael die?
I know not – taken from the place
was I before the story's end could see.
And thus, I must one day return
and see it through to story's end
for in me now a fire doth burn
and I would seek to comprehend
the lovers' tale, and how their end will be.

BOOK THE SECOND

THE SEER OF ALBION

PROLOGUE

I

But now return-ed to the earth
I lie upon my bed again
I have no sleep, for Attie's birth
and life, and love, and faith, and fame
present themselves before my face e'en now.
I toss and turn and walk the room.
I lie again in search of rest,
then cast my eyes upon the moon.
My heart beats urgent in my breast –
the end from the beginning I must know.

II

Now daylight comes, brings no relief,
and still I yearn within to know
if Attie lived ('tis my belief
that Michael died and she did go
to heav'n by choice to be with her love true).
But I did not the ending see
and falsehoods I refused to pen.
Full truthful I demand to be
and thus I must now go again
to astral plane to see the truth anew.

III

Thus, I shall summon Mercury
to fly to me from heav'nly home
and I will bid him carry me
(I cannot go there on my own)
unto the astral plane a second time.
That I should Attie spy anew
with Michael dead upon the ground
and learn the fate of lovers true
and whether life they now have found.
This story then I'll pen here line by line.

IV

But night's now come and I'm alone.
Full robbed of sleep I am once more.
I lie within my empty home,
I hear no footfall at the door
and none will come, it seems, to comfort me.
But wait! A sound of rushing winds
the thunder claps, the earth doth quake
the Wing-ed Messenger descends.
He roars a question – heavens shake –
"Tell who it is that summons Mercury."

V

"Winged Messenger – 'tis I, the Scribe.
I bid thee, let me see the end
– unfinished stories men deride.
To astral plane thou shalt me send
that I might write the end of love's true tale."
"Ahh, Scribe, 'tis meet that thou dost call
me to thy side again this night.
For though thou think'st to see it all
if thou wouldst tell the story right
'tis not the end that thou dost need to see…"

VI

"…but the beginning of this tale
that thou might understand it well.
And in thy duty do not fail
the final history to tell.
A revelation I shall make to thee.
So back in time we must engage
Full forty years and yet four more
to Seer's birth and parentage
and cross the sea to Albion's shore –
for thou must know his genealogy."

VII

Then drew he once again his sword
and lightning flashed and thunder rolled.
The wind did rush and surge abroad
around my waist he did take hold.
Then rose we, spun we, turned we in the night.
Thus in a flash we both were gone
and hurtled back. Through decades four
and four more years we have now flown
then found ourselves on Albion's shore –
a green and pleasant land of true delight.

I

THE SEER IS BORN

VIII

He took me to a market square
where men did trade and barter stock
and women cried to sell their wares
and shepherds tended to their flock.
A couple there he pointed out to me.
The woman, close to birth of child;
the man attentive to his wife
and she of disposition mild.
Together, they did make a life
a fam'ly in the making I could see.

IX

And when now her confinement came
she laid her back upon the bed.
Delivered she a child again
her second born, her gift of God
and named him Michael,'who is like the Lord'.
Her vision for the child she spake:
that he would grow in peace and grace
and unto him the lonely take
to set things rightly in their place
and thus be true – a simple son of God.

X

But in those days a plague did spread
upon the land of Albion
thus many died and men in dread
did cry for children who were torn
from mothers' breasts to lie within the earth.
The heart-cry from the land did rise
as many thousands took their leave.
The Reaper sets our time to die.
We have no choice if we should live –
no more than we can choose our date of birth.

XI

And in the little market town
where Mercury had taken me
the square was silent – most were gone
and lay now in the cemetery.
Amongst them, Michael's mother, father too.
But Michael lived and so did too
his sibling (not much older, she).
So they would start their lives anew
looked after by some family
and hoped that they could keep the truth in view.

XII

Thus, Michael learned from youngest days
that life is precious – guard it well!
Be careful, thou, in all thy ways
to use thy time for heav'n not Hell,
or curs-ed thou shall surely ever be.
'Tis sad but true that Michael went
to carer who was hard of heart.
Resented she that he was sent
to live with her, and from the start
did separate him from his sister brave.

XIII

And thus in isolation now
he did begin to walk his way.
Shut out from love he soon found how
to walk by night and sleep by day.
Exposure to the higher things he sought.
And feeling deep his destiny
(for nothing had he left below)
from in himself he soon would see,
discovering that he could go
to astral plane at will, as he would choose.

XIV

Now, when his carer learned of this
she schemed full evil in her heart
to profit deeply from this gift
and so arranged for him to part
and sold she him to bondage – slavery.
For thus she reasoned in her heart
I want him not. He is not mine
and he has not been from the start
so, if possessing power divine,
some profit I will see he shows to me.

XV

So, gold she did take for the boy
of tender years (just eight was he)
and in the money sought great joy
and thought that she fulfilled would be –
but realised not that evil yearnings kill.
And thus, within the year she caught
an illness strange, and none could say
why she did sicken in the heart
but very soon did pass away
in pain and sin; and went her soul to Hell.

XVI

The slaver who had bought the child
did know full well the gift he had
and thought that though he was but mild
a better price he'd surely yield
if sold directly at King Arthur's court.
For there were masters good and bad
of powers deep and deadly too
and many great resources had,
who'd prize a gifted child anew.
And thus by some magician he'd be bought.

XVII

In chains the slaver Michael brought
to Royal House of Albion.
And in the royal courtyard sought
a princely sum from some great man.
Thus, placed he him upon a pedestal.
But from the crowd a voice did rise:
"Unhand the child, thou evil knave
or I shall part the heavens' skies
(I hope thy heart is in the brave)
and summon demons to take thee to Hell."

XVIII

On hearing this did slaver flare
in rage to view his challenger.
But when he saw a beggar there
did deem him but a worthless cur
and laughed to scorn the warning he'd received.
He drew his sword and held it high
as if to strike a powerful blow
but when the beggar saw it nigh
he dropp-ed down his body low
and shifted shape (if this can be believed).

XIX

Then roaring tiger in his stead
the crowd did see and fast did part.
The slaver then was filled with dread
as tiger leapt straight for his heart
and tore it violent from within his breast.
The crowd did fly in panic wild
as tiger roared a victory cry
but Michael stood, his spirit mild,
and no escape did he then try,
for second sight had come at his behest...

XX

… to tell him he was safe with beast
and man, and thus he did contain
his fear whilst others now did feast
their panic at the thought of pain.
In terror fled they courtyard square that day.
When all were gone and it was still
the tiger turned unto the child
but meant no harm and would not kill,
composed itself in spirit mild,
and shifted shape again within its way.

XXI

Then stood the beggar in its stead
attired in rags and poverty.
He touched the boy upon the head
and asked him, "Child, dost thou fear me?
For terror I in many hearts do place."
Spake Michael now unto the man,
"Good sir, I see into thy heart.
I fear thee not since thou began
to stand for me and take my part
and freed me from the slave's life I did face."

XXII

"For whilst I now a beggar see
there is much more than thou hast shown.
And if a tiger thou canst be,
then stand before me as a man,
a mighty man of magic thou must be.
Thus I perceive thy power within
and surely I would learn of thee
the ways of wisdom to begin –
if thou are willing to teach me
and thoughts of childhood now I choose to flee.

XXIII

Then spake the beggar to the same,
"Now child, if thou a Seer be
look on my heart and speak my name
and tell me my identity
and if thou canst do this, then thou hast power.
And I shall take thee as my son
and teach thee all the ways I know
and thou shalt live within my home
– directly there we now shall go.
Thy learning shall begin this very hour."

XXIV

Then Michael lifted up his eyes,
on heaven did he fix his gaze;
the beggar's test did not despise
and stared into the violet haze;
Then lifted up his voice to speak the name.
"Good sir, thou know'st I look on heart
and not on flesh that men present
and thou dost know that from the start
I looked on thee as heaven-sent
My saviour Merlin, thou art he – the same!

XXV

Then beggar lifted hands up high
and pointed up to heaven's gate
the clouds did part as he did cry,
"Indeed, child, thou hast truly spake
my name and art a Seer of the heart.
Thus rise we now to astral plane
where I shall teach thee of my ways
and oft we shall return again
and in this place will spend our days
in service to the good of Arthur's court."

XXVI

And thus it was at eight years old
did Michael now his learning start,
developing his powers bold
and always seeing in the heart,
the truth of men he rightly did discern.
Of many ways then learn-ed he
that did the wizard now him teach
of spells, and powers and alchemy
such unto heaven he could reach
and thus as he did grow, so he did learn.

XXVII

His 'prenticeship took twenty year
and in that time he learned full well
as always did the boy defer
to mentor – Merlin – for his spell
and power and righteousness he wished to learn.
Thus as he grew in strength and sense
and took upon him magic skill
full well he grew in confidence
and powers of darkness sought to quell.
Thus, for true wisdom did he daily yearn.

XXVIII

A frequent visitor was he
with Merlin to King Arthur's court
where whispers were of alchemy
and magic powers of darker sort.
But Michael treated astral plane as home.
In many wars the boy took part
supporting righteousness and truth
in Arthur's cause he took great heart
and in God's ways he spent his youth
till thirty years of Michael's life had gone.

II

THE ELFIN WARS

XXIX

Arthurian territ'ry was fraught
as elfin powers from Ob'ron's land
and gremlins of still darker sort
would take to combat hand-to-hand
with Arthur's knights to gain the upper part.
But always Arthur's men would quell
incursions from the elfin land
because they all could surely tell
upon which borders elves did stand
their greatest forces from the very start.

XXX

The elfin lords confus-ed were
as how the humans always knew
the very place where they'd incur
and were they many or were few
the elfin forces men would surely quell.
The reason why they could not learn
and caus-ed it great argument
amongst the lords who each did yearn
(and not one of them would repent)
the secret for to know and first to tell.

XXXI

For Ob'ron roared in elfin court
and beat his breast and howled in rage,
that if the secret would be taught
to him and thus his thirst assuage
for human blood and human territ'ry,
the one who first would speak the truth
and tell him why the humans won
to him he would restore his youth –
renewed again he would become
With magic costly, bless-ed he would be.

XXXII

Then lord did vie with lord alike
to know the secret of the power
and thus give Ob'ron strength to strike
the humans at the witching hour
and elves would surely take Arthurian court.
But none could guess the Seer true
who did their hearts so clearly see
and thus could speak their plans anew
ensuring they would thwarted be,
as Merlin did the knights with power support.

XXXIII

Thus, Michael worked with Merlin. Fast
their powers did grow in sympathy.
The one would see the other cast
his spells and knights would bless-ed be
when clash-ed they with elfin troops again.
And thus, it seemed that it would be
a human right to win the wars
and keep this bless-ed territ'ry.
Eleven years without a pause
they elfin troops did constantly disdain.

XXXIV

But curses (and I tell the truth)!
– a traitor rose in human group.
A sapling boy, a mere frail youth
the least of Arthur's mighty troop
had honours sought, but had been turned away.
Resentment burned within his heart
and he would now aveng-ed be
with crucial secret he would part
and tell of Michael who could see
and human 'vantage would he thus defray.

XXXV

The boy (one Alfred) now did steal
from human camp at dead of night
his darkest purpose: to reveal
the secret of King Arthur's might
to Oberon and thus aveng-ed be.
And so he came to elfin camp
and spoke up boldly in his cause
to elfin soldier of low rank,
"Pray tell me, elf, and make no pause
how mighty Ob'ron I can come to see."

XXXVI

The elfin sentry turned in fright!
His sword he drew, protecting him
from human threat, and he would fight.
Confronting boy, he did begin
to parry and to thrust at Alfred's heart.
Then cried the youth, "I come in peace
no quarrel do I have with thee
so quickly give thy heart relief
and I to thee no threat will be.
To Ob'ron I must speak and then depart."

XXXVII

The sentry called for helpers three
and plac-ed they the boy in chains.
And thus they could purport to be
brave soldiers who dark threats disdain.
Then dragg-ed they the youth to Oberon's tent.
They forced him down upon his knees,
and Alfred, then he did repent
his treacherous thoughts and tendencies
but too late now his honour to reclaim.

XXXVIII

Then Oberon drew out his sword
and, placing it at throat of youth,
spake harshly and these were the words:
"Speak, human, and speak only truth
or thou shalt die in tortuous agony.
Why hast thou come unto my camp
Does Arthur now send out a boy?
A feeble sapling has he sent
and art thou come here as a spy?
And wilt thou speak of what thou dost now see?"

XXXIX

Then trembled Alfred at these words
and felt his heart within him weep.
And shook-ed he at Oberon's sword
and softer part he now did seek.
Then with these words his cause he now did tell.
"Great captain, I hold secrets deep
of Arthur's strength and of his power.
And I intelligence would seek
to bring to thee now at this hour.
And for this I know I am cursed to Hell."

XL

"What is thy secret, foolish youth?"
Cried Ob'ron at his boyish fears
"And if thou dost not tell the truth
then run-ed through with elfin spears
thy heart shall be within thy wretched frame."
The boy, he prostrated himself
at Oberon's feet and cried and wept:
"Kill not me, Sir, thou honoured elf
though now, of honour, I'm bereft.
I seek to save my life, sir, just the same."

XLI

"The secret I have come to tell
brings great advantage to thy cause
concerning mighty magic spell
and where the King his power draws
to quell incursions into Albion.
For Arthur has the same as thee
by way of troops and war machine
and yet, his forces are now free
to counter thine – and hast thou seen
the magic of the way that this is done?"

XLII

"For Arthur has supporting him
two men of magic – pow'rful sorts.
The first, he doth see deep within
and is full clear of thy purport
and where thou dost thine elfin troops deploy.
The second – Merlin – casts a spell
on Albion's knights as they do seek
to drive thy soldiers back full well
to elfin borders as we speak.
And thus, in Arthur's camp, is ever joy."

XLIII

"Hence, fearing nought they do prevail
by cause of magic men's support
who, though they be in body frail,
are deep revered in Arthur's court.
In inner sight and magic are they bold.
Now, furthermore (mark this full well)
these men who guide his destiny
does Arthur keep safe – true to tell,
to thy success they hold the key.
The very keys to Albion do they hold!"

XLIV

The elf, he pondered thoughtfully,
considering if the boy spoke true
for if he did, then this could be
a means of vanquishing anew
the power of men throughout all Albion.
Thus spake he softly at that hour,
"Pray tell me now, if thou dost know,
the name of Seer, man of power
who doth cause Arthur's might to grow.
Speak truly and let all thy fears be gone."

XLV

Now, Alfred knew he'd said too much
and if he gave the elf the name
t'would power grant and elves would touch
the source of Arthur's strength and gain
the means to take his magic full away.
But feared he more for his own life
and elfin sword still at his breast
and elfin troops about him, rife,
and thus he chose now to divest
himself of final secret on that day.

XLVI

"The Seer, Michael is his name,
deep, pow'rful sight possesses he.
He lives upon the astral plane
where he and Merlin's spirits be
and pow'rful magic do they there compose.
From thither they to Gaia fly
to Arthur's cause they are full true
and righteousness they glorify
and each day brings them power anew.
'Tis thus the King can vanquish all his foes."

XLVII

The elf considered this at length
Again he pondered in deep thought,
that if the cause of Arthur's strength
was truly with such magic wrought
then vanquished would his kingdom be anew.
At last he roused him from his trance
and gazed he on the sallow youth.
Then Oberon pick-ed up a lance
and spake unto the boy uncouth:
"Frail human, hast thou heard my promise true?"

XLVIII

"That to the one who did disclose
the source of Arthur's pow'r to me
to him I'd grant a treasure trove
– restored to him his youth would be.
Now unto thee thy youth I shall enhance.
For thou already dost have youth
and art though a mere sapling tree
I'll make thee young – see now my truth...
when thou shalt reincarnate be!"
And then he ran the boy through with the lance.

XLIX

The child, he clutch-ed at his heart.
His eyes were wide, his life did spill
and Oberon smiled for his part
for he did love the human kill –
and pleasure took-ed he in death that day.
His court, approval, murmured then
to watch their King despatch the boy
and from that point did they begin
their confidence now to employ
that Arthur's power they soon would steal away.

III

THE COMING OF THE DRAGON

I.

Then Ob'ron did with lords confer
to settle how this truth they'd use.
But each did to their King defer
in case their leader did accuse
them of some evil foolishness that day.
Thus, Ob'ron pondered through the night
when all was quiet and dark around
of ways to counter Arthur's might
and make his own power to abound
by count'ring Michael's sight in some strange way.

LI

Then daylight stole across the plain
where elfin tents were pitched for war
and Oberon did rise again
and pondered long on ancient lore
and thus, a plan did to his mind occur.
Then call-ed he unto his side
the elfin lords he did control
and thus he spake with greatest pride
and told the contents of his soul –
and all did with his mighty plan concur.

LII

"My lords, I see no point today
in sending elves to Albion.
The Seer will see – come what may
and Arthur's troops will win again.
A subtler, deeper plan do we require.
'Tis my decision in my heart
that deepest powers of Hell be called
I'll ask them to lend me support
and thus shall Michael be enthralled.
Deception now shall underpin my power!"

LIII

The Elvin lords did acquiesce
in Ob'ron's plan (though all did fear
lest their great King could not redress
the powers he summoned loud and clear
and Hellish strength would be let loose that day).
But none looked into Ob'ron's eyes
to challenge what their King had wrought
lest mighty leader should despise
their caution and their fearful thought.
And thus did all unto the King give way.

LIV

Then Oberon called for witches three,
to summon from the darkest Hell
the dragon known as Harmony
who took form also as a girl,
a human woman full of piety.
And thus he schemed within this guise
to send the dragon forth from there.
She would distract the Seer's eyes
preventing him from making war.
Besotted with a lover he would be.

LV

Then in the dark the witches danced
around a cauldron, casting spells.
And when they all were lost in trance
they called in unison to Hell
"Dark mistress! From the depths we summon thee!
Come hither to thy servants here
a boon we now would ask of thee
and to thee make our purpose clear.
We call thee, mighty Harmony!
Thy power loosed on the earth we now would see."

LVI

Then from the boiling cauldron came
a fiery flame of deepest red.
The witches did convulse in pain
and fell now as if they were dead
as flame and cloud – it from the cauldron poured.
And then a rumbling deep within
its frame began. And louder now
the sound grew harsh and did begin
to shake with voice of greatest power
"Now! Who unleashes Harmony abroad?"

LVII

Then from the cauldron did emerge
at witches' call and their behest,
with power and energy did surge,
a single serpent's head with crest
of horn – and eyes that deep with hate did gleam.
It glared around at all that lay
before it on the earthen floor.
Prostrated on the ground all they
save Ob'ron standing at the door
who stood with confidence before the scene.

LVIII

"Who calleth Harmony?" it said
again as round about it stared.
"For that one now shall wish him dead
unless he be in truth prepared
to satisfy a dragon come from Hell."
Then Ob'ron lifted up his voice
in confidence he did speak forth,
"I call thee, Harmony, by choice.
And though I deem thy power of worth
I do require that thou shall serve me well."

LIX

"The service I do seek of thee
– thou shalt take pleasure in the task.
For if thou now wilt come with me
and will put on thy human mask
I satisfaction now to thee shall bring.
A Seer do I offer thee –
from Albion – King Arthur's court.
Though he a mild man seems to be,
with second sight great deeds hath wrought.
Destroying such as this makes thy heart sing.

LX

The serpent bowed its head in thought.
It seemed as if to contemplate,
as if uncertainty had caught
it unaware, and it did make
to leave that place and unto Hell return.
Then finally it lifted up
it eyes to Oberon and spake:
"'Tis my decision now to sup
and of this cup I shall partake
for human hatred in my heart doth burn."

LXI

Then thunder came from cauldron now
and six more heads they did ooze forth
all dripping venom, caustic flow,
as dragon now did show its wrath
and rose up from the smoke unto the room.
Its evil body – scaly, green,
with dragon wings it was adorned.
Great evilness, it now was seen,
and witches three quaked, all forlorn
as if they now prepared to meet their doom.

LXII

Then dragon stare-ed in the eye
the elfin King who by it stood
and then did lunge with dragonish cry
and tore apart the witches' brood
and dragged each witch's body from her head.
And then without a second glance
upon the death that it had wrought
the dragon stood as if to pounce
upon the elf, so that his court
would know their elfin King was truly dead.

LXIII

But dragon did not King attack.
Instead it stood in front of him;
and with its tail did cauldron crack
and thus could no one now begin
to send it back to Hell whence it had come.
Then as it stood before the elf
it smiled at him with softer eye
and now before him did begin
to shift its shape and, by the by,
a maiden stood unclothed and all alone.

IV
DRAGON LOVE

LXIV

Full beauteous she, and soft of face,
her hair was flaxen gold and long,
a perfect specimen of grace
so human that my heart took song
to sing the wondrous creature I beheld.
And though I knew 'twas dragon true
I could not but believe the lie
and I could tell what she would do
to make the Seer full comply
with evil will of serpent come from Hell.

LXV

"Come, slaves!" commanded Oberon
"And bring the lady robes, I say
that she and I might soon be gone.
And when the light of dawning day
doth fall upon the elfin camp once more,
we shall fly to the astral plane
where Seer lives and makes his home
and when he doth come there again,
and when we find him all alone,
sweet Harmony shall with his heart confer."

LXVI

The human slaves of elfin King
did hurry to the raiment store
and to the maiden now did bring
the choicest robes, and jewels, more
than any maiden ever could desire.
But maiden lifted up her voice
commanding, "Nay! It shall not be.
A ruder garment is my choice.
Bedecked with jewels I'll not be
my beauty only shall his heart inspire."

LXVII

Then maiden dressed in garments plain
and put about her waist a belt.
Her dress, unto her knees it came,
and yet her beauty still could melt
the coldest heart that ever did her spy.
Then Oberon and Harmony
set forth unto the astral plane
and then they did seek sanctuary
to wait till Michael came again
and then seek to deceive him with the lie.

LXVIII

Now lodged upon the astral plane,
the maiden and the evil elf
did wait till Michael came again
and from the battle ease himself
(for second sight did drain the Seer deep).
As type to type will always draw,
the maiden sought herself a place
both dank and dark, a dragon's lair,
that would not suit a heart of grace
and then she did await the Seer meek.

LXIX

Then Ob'ron to his troops returned
and maiden waited on alone
while hatred deep within her burned
(for humankind her love was gone).
What caused the hatred, I could not yet say.
But patiently she kept her peace
and focusing on Seer mild
did plan his downfall and demise
by her he would now be beguiled.
His life she surely meant to take away.

LXX

Three days and nights attended she
and waited for the man to come.
Her patience would rewarded be
when Michael did return to home –
and then she heard a footfall at his gate.
His soul was caught in weariness
and now good sleep his body craved.
For, though a man of gentleness,
the thick of battle had he braved
to add his inner eye to Arthur's might.

LXXI

Thus did he stumble to his home
and on his bed full dressed did fall.
Deep slumber did he seek alone,
a resting place, and that was all,
to take some peace from battle deep within.
Then Harmony did see her chance
and right unto his bedside came
and on him place the deepest trance
that when he woke he'd feel the same
despite the spell that she would cast on him.

LXXII

The dawn did come and in its light,
the Seer rose from slumber deep.
And as it was the end of night,
to quench his thirst he now did seek
and thus unto the well he now did come.
And there he spied sweet Harmony
who, girt about in raiment rude,
a picture, she, of probity,
and thus the Seer did conclude,
his business there and started out for home.

LXXIII

But then his progress check-ed he
and came he to the well again.
And he would speak to Harmony
(though knew he not it was her name).
A powerful spell had turned his head that day.
For though the Seer sought not youth
or beauty in the maiden fair,
he looked upon the heart, in truth,
and when he looked, what he saw there
– or thought he saw – did his concern repay.

LXXIV

For when he looked upon her heart
great sadness did he seem to see
as if from love she once did part
(and joy for her was not to be)
but now had set her mind on other ways.
He spoke unto the maiden, sweet:
"Good lady, pray, what saddens thee?
Thy countenance – it seems not meet
for one of youth and strength to be
so melancholic in these summer days."

LXXV

"For youth should be a time of joy
and dance should be thy favoured part
but thou dost not thyself employ
in joyful matters of the heart.
Thy spirit weighs, like lead, within thy breast.
So tell me why and I'll assist
thee to find light and joy again
and from thy sadness now desist
embrace thy happiness and then
take thou thy part in pleasure like the rest."

LXXVI

"For here upon the astral plane
'tis clear to me that thou art one
who does the joys of youth disdain
and surely here thou art now come
in search of satisfaction to thy soul.
It is not common now for one
of youth and beauty such as thee
to make this magic place her home
and I surmise from what I see
that thou art come here now to be made whole."

LXXVII

Then gazed he into maiden's heart
and did not know that by her spell
protected she her deeper part
wherein her darker self did dwell
and all he saw he took as it did seem.
Then, lifted up now, Harmony,
her voice as honey-sweetened dew.
She spoke to Seer carefully
and chose her words, they were but few:
"Good sir, my story now to thee I tell."

LXXVIII

And at that the voice did Seer turn
for loveliness he did perceive
of spirit and his heart did yearn
for female virtues such as she
did have, and strength he there did see as well.
Then something deep in him did move.
Though time he had not previously
found for the like of woman-love
at age of forty-one thought he
to dwell alone, as Merlin did foretell.

LXXIX

Enthral-ed was he at her voice
as she began to speak and tell.
Thus sat he with her by his choice
and spent the day beside the well
entranced and taken by this woman fair.
And all the while in easy grace
with words of great felicity
she told the story of her place
and purpose there in history.
Thus deemed he her a maid beyond compare.

LXXX

She told him of her Gaian home.
In far-off Freedom did she dwell
and how she had long lived alone
in isolation. He could tell
the life that she did choose was solit'ry.
A woman of great learning, she
who spent her time within her books
of mind had great ability
and cared she not for facial looks
her beauty little meant to Harmony.

LXXXI

And as the sun did o'er them set
and shadows lengthened by the well
the Seer felt they must have met
in former life. 'Tis true to tell
he lost his heart to Harmony that day.
Then with the darkness she did leave
and Michael sat the whole night through
possessed was he, he did perceive
of deepest passion and of love
and in control of this he had no say.

LXXXII

There sat he till the sun did rise
and daylight broke through beck'ning trees
and all the while he did surmise
of reasons why her heart did grieve –
how he for her a new joy might create.
Then as the sun to zenith came
did Harmony once more return
and though she looked still just the same
from her own lips he sought to learn
if she his feelings did reciprocate.

LXXXIII

The maiden shyly smiled at him
and reach-ed for the Seer's hand.
And thus these two did now begin
to walk abroad upon the land.
And touching soul to soul they did that day
begin their passions to awake.
And Seer was distracted now
– no further thought he then did take
of human battles far below
nor of the grievous error of his way.

LXXXIV

Then as the days turned into weeks
they true companions did become
and each the other oft did seek
as if their love, now once begun,
full consummate then it must surely be.
No thought had they that time did fly
as they their lovers' trysts did make
nor how it was that, by the by,
that others did their absence take
as sign of grievous infidelity.

V

THE DRAGON TURNS

LXXXV

Thus, in the elfin camp I saw
King Ob'ron, of emotions mixed
as rapidly he paced the floor
and waited for the dragon-witch
to come with news of Seer's full demise.
But while his troops incursions made
deep into Arthur's Albion
and second sight they could evade
(for human 'vantage now was gone),
still did he carry anger deep inside.

LXXXVI

His heart cried out for Seer's death
a hater, he, of humankind
and sought to leave them full bereft
of second sight from Michael's mind
and wished to see him fin'lly in his grave.
But still no word from Harmony
did come his way to tell him true
as he had asked repeatedly
that she should place within his view
the Seer's heart and not his body save...

LXXXVII

...or spare his life for pity's sake
but end his being finally.
Thus, Oberon resolved to make
a further trip to Harmony –
and to the astral plane did he revert.
He there confronted in her cave
the dragon form of Harmony:
"Now, why the Seer dost thou save
when I have said repeatedly
thou must the cause of righteousness pervert?"

LXXXVIII

The dragon merged to human form
and maiden did confront the King
and in her eyes he saw, forlorn,
the depths of passion deep within.
For Harmony did now the Seer love.
"Thou fool," he quoth in angry voice
"Thou dost of human love partake?
And of the Seer make a choice
thus with this human love to make?
Thy lover's head before me I shall have!"

LXXXIX

Then maiden now as dragon spoke:
"Be warn-ed now King Oberon
that I shall not my pledge revoke
– he'll be removed from Albion –
for Harmony doth always keep her word.
But be thou well advised, Elf-king
another promise do I make:
that if thou harm'st one hair of him
thine own dear life will Harm'ny take
and strew thy hapless body far abroad."

XC

"'Tis true that I do love a man
unique in all humanity
and yes, I did take dragon form
as surely thou canst clearly see
when as a woman I had thought love lost.
And yes, I gave my soul to Hell
and did forget my human ways.
An elf like thee could never tell
that I once spent in human days
a life of passion – but did count the cost."

XCI

"A former love was took from me
I watched his body torn apart
by Albion's men. Then I did see
no other way to 'venge his part
than I myself a dragon form to take.
And long was I condemned to Hell
for grievous sin I did commit.
My dragon form did pay them well
– I took them with me to the pit
where even now in torture they partake…"

XCII

"…of Hell's own bowers and demon joy
and play with devils do they make
and I their suffering did enjoy
and did once satisfaction take
that they did pay the price for evil deeds.
But when thou didst call unto me,
I did not know that when I came
I would, of Hell, be set full free
nor that I then could love again
when in my human form from dragon freed."

XCIII

"So be advised, thou elfin King,
that I shall take the Seer's sight
but I shall never now begin
his life to threaten with my might.
For now his soul is precious unto me.
So be thou gone, thou evil elf,
and play with human politics
but keep this story to thyself –
do not attempt thine elfin tricks
or thou shalt face the wrath of Harmony."

XCIV

The elf, he sought to counter her,
but check-ed he his foremost thought.
He did to dragon power defer
and flew in anger to his court
(he knew her power was greater than his own).
And there, into a rage did fly,
and elfin lords in terror flew.
For no one in that court did try
to make King Ob'ron calm anew.
But wisely did they leave their King alone.

VI
DEEP MAGIC WROUGHT IN HISTORY

XCV

Now, all the while that this did pass
the Seer slept in perfect peace
and rose with dawn to come at last
unto the well for his release.
In Harmony he sought his solace true.
And there he found his lover gone.
No word left she of where she went.
Then by the well he waited long
in hope that she some note had sent
to say that she would come on morn anew.

XCVI

But when the dusk did cross the skies
and she'd not come to be with him
'twas then at last he did surmise
(for something told him deep within)
that Harmony was gone. And he alone
would be upon the astral plane
and she would not be at his side
and never would he be the same.
She would not now with him abide.
In sorrow deep return-ed he to home.

XCVII

And there, at last, he cried his fears
and wept he thus his heart away.
A river made he of his tears
and howl-ed he til coming day
did steal across the plane to bring the dawn.
But in the light he found no rest
and wept yet more to vent his pain
For he was now of love bereft
and knew she would not come again.
Thus he would now once more dwell all alone.

XCVIII

Then, as he lay and did begin
In deepest soul-ache now to writhe,
once more did Harm'ny come to him
(in vision only I surmise)
and plac-ed she her hands upon his eyes.
"Sleep now, my love," she softly spake –
caressed his cheek, her love still true.
"For I must now thy vision take
in order that I might heal you
and save you from those that would take your life."

XCIX

Then Michael into slumber fell
and rest did fin'lly come to him
as she did cast her deepest spell
he felt her presence deep within
and took-ed he some comfort in her love.
And as he slept she looked at him
deep tenderness within her heart
but for the greatness of her sin
she knew that she must now depart
and he would dwell below – and she above.

C

Then him she sent to Albion
and on the astral plane did make
her home, but from him sight was gone
and thus his vision did she take
from Michael, so that he'd at last be safe.
He would not know the truth of her
but think her simply gone from him
and to this last lie would defer
that he could start his life again.
She did not know this loss his heart would break.

CI

When Michael did awake he found
himself in court at Albion
and great confusion did surround
the question of where he had been.
But Merlin kept his counsel to himself.
For he had seen from vision deep
the history I now have told
and thus determined he would seek
a confrontation and be bold
and raise the matter with the evil elf.

CII

And thus to elfin camp he flew
in owlish form at dead of night
and there he did confront anew
the elfin King. And all his might
did powerful Merlin treat with almost mirth.
"Thou foolish elf, what has thou done?
For I see thy duplicity
in raising from the depths of Hell
the evil dragon Harmony.
And now Hell is let loose upon the earth."

CIII

"For neither power of elf nor man
will demon-dragon might contain
such magic from since time began
do fools like thee treat with disdain
and place our souls in peril – by my word.
And dost thou think to justify
thine actions and thine evil heart
because the dragon dost now fly
and from the earth it did depart
so thou couldst put my kingdom to the sword?"

CIV

"Thou fool. No human voice could speak
the idiocy that thou hast done.
Now a solution must I seek
in magic from the dawn of time
if I that foolish act am to contain.
And thus back into history
I have to fly at my great cost
to free the world from Harmony
or all our souls will now be lost
and at thy peril thou my words disdain."

CV

"I shall now fly to Freedom's land
and back into its history
and there shall seek till I have found
the purest being I can see.
And over many years must groom her true.
For only thus by my own hand
with preparations deep and long
can I begin to save the land
and thus ensure that dragonsong
will not upon the earth find voice anew."

CVI

Then spake the elf, "I hate thee well,
thou human wizard. Thou hast spoke,
and these thy plans that thou dost tell
by my own hand I will revoke.
Be warn-ed that my power is great as thine".
Then Merlin roared and mak-ed smoke
and rose he high into the air.
"Thou knave!" he cried. "Think'st to revoke
the truth that I have now made clear?
Beware – my power will always thine outshine."

CVII

And with these words he did depart
to travel back in history
and at a lake would find a heart
of deepest love and purity
and to that princess teach her warrior ways.
But not a moment later did
the elf, the wizard now pursue,
and Merlin's purpose was not hid
from him, and thus now did he view
the birth of Attie and her early days.

CVIII

Such that he did within himself
decide the little girl to take
and in her stead would place an elf
and take the child, and mischief make.
Thus Merlin's purposes would he now thwart.
But as I told in former tale
the wizard had foreseen this deed
and thus upon her placed a spell
and covered her within her need
to grow in peace and champion Judges' court.

CIX

And thus the story I have told
as Merc'ry showed it unto me
of knights and of magicians bold
and also of duplicity.
So now my heart lies quiet within my breast.
For though the story is not done
some understanding do I have
of how these things to pass did come
And now of thee I take my leave.
Another book shall tell thee all the rest.

BOOK THE THIRD

DRAGONSONG

PROLOGUE

I

Exhausted I now lay me down
and ponder in my deepest self
on acts of men of great renown,
of kingdoms, human and of elf,
and wonder if the ending I will find.
Now shall I summon Mercury
to come beside me once again
and once more make my eyes to see
still further truth, so I might then
the world of good and evil now remind?

II

For though the deeds that I have seen
I set forth here in clearest truth,
reminded I have always been
(and this has been so from my youth)
to speak of moral choices that we make.
Thus, as I write I'm full aware
the contents of these many books
do challenge us and make full clear
as each within his heart now looks
to ponder on the steps that we do take.

III

For each one treads his path of choice
and many footsteps do we leave
on others' lives when we find voice
or speak, and of our wisdom give
the 'benefit' to those that round us dwell.
For me, my task I clarify
I am not here to preach to thee
but thine own thoughts to amplify
that through these stories thou might'st see
and better light thy way to Heav'n or Hell.

IV

Thus I do ponder through the night
and now expect the Messenger
to come again in power and might
and once again to take me far
to past, or future, or across the sea.
For now I know he will reveal
the ending of this mighty tale
and on the story place his seal.
For though my telling is but frail,
now, this the final book shall surely be.

V

And yet I hear no rushing wind
no thunderclaps above me sound
so can it be that he'll descend
and place his feet upon the ground
or shall I sleep the whole night through alone?
But without warning, he is here –
yet seated he, upon my bed;
his might does not invoke my fear;
I fall not now as if I'm dead
so can it be that Mercury's power is gone?

VI

He speaks to me in softer tone,
"Hail, Scribe! I come again to thee."
He has no anger, but has grown
more weary since I him did see,
and now his heart is heavy in his breast.
"I come to thee from home of gods –
you humans give it many names;
Olympus, Asgard – matters not
to gods the terms are all the same.
So use the name thou think'st does fit it best."

VII

"The gods have seen thy writings, Scribe
and many issues do they stir.
And god with god doth now take side
in such a way as ne'er before
was seen amongst immortals of my kind.
And though we have debated long
in anger and in milder speech,
we fear now, greatly, dragonsong
unto the heavens could now reach
and earthly chaos would it leave behind."

VIII

"Thus I am charged to come to thee
and tell thee more than I think wise
but other gods do disagree
and call for wisdom from thee, Scribe.
And so, a story I will now unfold
of how the world of elves and man
did come about with heaven's support;
and when the kingdoms were begun
and how the magic first was wrought.
I tell thee, Scribe, this tale has ne'er been told."

IX

"But when I'm done and thou dost see
I'll charge thee with a moral choice,
for god with god doth disagree
and none doth have ascendant voice
on how to end this tale that is begun.
For moral choices men have made
and elves did too participate
and thus cannot seek to evade
the consequences, but must take
responsibility for dragonsong."

X

"And so the gods do ask of thee
that when thou know'st the story's start
thou take responsibility
and look, then, into thine own heart
and make a final ending to this tale.
We promise thee, oh human scribe,
whichever ending thou dost set
and doth within a book describe,
the gods of Asgard now will let
that ending to the story full prevail."

XI

I looked upon the Messenger
could'st scarce believe what he did say –
the gods would trust a human cur
and him allow a part to play
and to decide the fate of humankind!
But then my heart rose in my breast.
I set myself unto the task
and knew that I could take no rest
until the ending came at last.
And strength for this decision I would find.

XII

"Great Mercury, I hear thy words
and of this task I shall partake.
And if it be required by gods
then this decision I shall make
when thou hast told the story to me here.
For thou dost rightly to me say
I need to see the history
preceding what I know today
that I might now enlightened be
and make my moral choice whilst full aware."

XIII

"But one thing I must ask of thee –
The dragon thou didst show me slain;
yet now fear dragonsong will be
at gates of Asgard heard again.
Pray tell me of this strange phenomenon."
"Ahh, Scribe," replied then Mercury,
"thou think'st a dragon can be slain?
I tell thee, nay, and thou must see
that such a beast doth rise again.
Forever doth eternal life go on."

XIV

"A dragon's not a mortal beast,
for it from hell did surely come.
And thou canst not stop in the least
the rising power of dragonsong
unless the dragon does itself concur.
And thus thou must determine fate
of dragon and of humankind,
and in thy tale must now relate,
and a solution must thou find.
Then Asgard will unto thy choice defer."

XV

"Now Mercury, set forth thy tale,
and I, the Scribe, a book shall make,
that good o'er evil shall prevail
in moral choices I shall take.
But first I need to know the history.
Then shall it be that I shall write
two books before my task is done.
This first shall be writ from thy sight.
The second work shall from me come.
Speak, Messenger —and make my eyes to see!"

XVI

Then Mercury took deepest breath
to speak up in soliloquy.
He stood before me, pale as death,
and in his eyes I now could see
the torment of his immortality.
"Yea, Scribe, now listen to my words
and full consider what I say
that gods may put away their swords
for violence should not be our way
and now I shall set forth thy history."

I
HISTORY SET FORTH

XVII

There was a time when o'er the earth
walked gods with men and elfin kind
together made we greatest mirth
and thoughts of war filled not our mind
but all did live as one in harmony.
A golden age of peace did reign
and love, it dwelt in every breast
and men and gods and elves the same
would take the actions all thought best
and each sought merely life to live full free.

XVIII

Then selfishness did enter in
and each sought an identity
and thus we slowly did begin
to take our dwellings separately.
Thus gods and men and elves did dwell apart.
The gods to Asgard did remove;
the elves went unto Elfindom,
and unto men it was behove
to choose the kingdoms for their own.
Three kingdoms men established from the start.

XIX

The men of east did Norsedane start;
the central kingdom, Albion;
and to the west was Freedom's part
where Lady Attie made her home.
Thus all men then did live in kingdoms three.
The gods did ponder in their home
the governance of human ways
and did determine they alone
would set the course and length of days
of man and elves who dwelt in harmony.

XX

The gods determined in their heart
that man five hundred years would live.
And elves would take a better part
for unto them the gods would give
a double time span than was granted man.
As to the kingdoms' governance
the gods determined it was meet,
the ways of man now to enhance
and set a person who'd entreat
the Kings and Princes that did rule them then.

XXI

The title that they gave to them
was 'Judges'. Them they did endow
(as did befit such special men)
with powers, and they did mark their brow
with magic signs that set such ones apart.
In Norsedane was one Judge alone
and Vidar was the name he'd take.
In Albion (where lions roam)
'twas Merlin, that the earth would shake.
But Freedom's land was different from the start.

XXII

In Norsedane and in Albion
did kings arise from ranks of man
who ruled when Judges left their home
to go to Asgard, or began
to meditate their minds within themselves.
But Freedom sought no kings to head
them in the same way, but did take
four Judges unto them instead
and thus these four did justice make
and also dealt with other kings and elves.

XXIII

Faith, Love and True Equality
are titles known unto thy mind.
The fourth was titled Harmony.
And now thou think'st that thou dost find
the ending of my story from the start.
But wait! Hold back thy judgment now
for there is much more I must tell.
'tis needful for me to show how
a path the dragon took to Hell
that thou might'st judge correctly from thy heart.

XXIV

But also be aware, full well,
that Elfindom, it was not ruled,
by Judges, and the truth I tell –
the elfin people would not yield
to aught but mighty rulers of their own.
And thus arose in Elfindom
abrasive rulers, pow'rful sorts
called Captain-Kings, and they did come
to rule by might in elfin court
and all elves did defer to them alone.

XXV

The greatest of the Captain-Kings
was Mordain, Lord of day and night.
He was reputed to have wings
and flight enhanced his pow'r and might;
and unto Mordain was there born a son.
And thus he ruled his kingdom well,
this Captain-King, this elf of might,
beloved of elves, we thus could tell
he ruled his kingdom true and right;
and named he then his son as Oberon.

XXVI

Now in the land of Albion
did Merlin rule and judge aright
and unto him strong men did come
to learn of magic power and might.
Thus fame of Merlin's deeds was spread abroad.
And when repute of magic power
had come unto the elfin court
did Mordain counsel take that hour.
Thus he did wish his son be taught
of magic power by man of righteous word.

XXVII

The elfin lords, they did concur;
and delegation then was sent
to take the word they would defer
to human Judge, and provident
decision of the kingdom was now made;
that Oberon would thus be sent
to learn at feet of magic Judge
and this the elves would not repent
and nor could any now begrudge
the gain the child would make by human aid.

XXVIII

And many hoped that by this step
a new alliance would be forged;
that elves and man would not regret
but kingdoms both would be enlarged
in understanding and in harmony.
But Oberon had not been asked
if he desired in heart to go
to human world as he was tasked
to learn of magic rites, and know
the ways of Merlin that he soon would see.

XXIX

Thus in his heart resentment grew
against King Mordain and his court.
But covered he this, well and true,
and thought it was a better part
to go and learn, developing his power.
And when he had amassed such might
of magic as he felt he could
then planned he to return at night,
confront his father, then he would
the kingdom seize and rule it at that hour.

II

TO MERLIN, A DAUGHTER

XXX

Thus Oberon did now set forth
with servants three, and train in tow.
And thus he came to Albion's court
the ways of Merlin now to know.
His sojourn there one hundred years would be.
Now Merlin was a man of might
but softness held he in his heart
and thus considered he it right
whilst he was young to make a start
to find a wife and found a dynasty.

XXXI

The maid that he took unto him
fair Allyson, as she was known,
with tender eyes she did begin
to love him and make him a home.
Then rested he from judging Albion.
And in due time did Allyson
a child bring forth from in her womb.
Though Merlin did desire a son
the daughter born into his home
he took to him and loved her, his firstborn.

XXXII

Then in the night he carried her
in owlish form to Asgard then
presented he, and did defer
to Nanna and did then begin
to seek her blessing on his daughter fair.
Then thus spake Nanna unto him
in deepest words of prophecy,
"Good Merlin, thou must soon begin
(for danger do I clearly see)
to teach thy daughter ways of magic here."

XXXIII

"Rebekah, thou shalt call her name
and greatest power I see in her.
Be watchful of the elf that came
and never now to him defer
or else he will thy daughter greatly harm.
For she is precious unto thee
protect her well from dangers now.
Enhance her powers that she might be
thy helper and in magic grow
and unto thee become a soothing balm."

XXXIV

Now Merlin paid the greatest heed
unto the words the goddess spoke
and in himself he felt a need
thus Ob'ron's learning to revoke
but could not, for the sake of Albion.
For elves and men dwelt side by side
and such an action would destroy
the peace that now did long abide
and men and elves would thus employ
the tools of war, and evil would be done.

XXXV

Thus, took he 'Bekah back with him
and placed her safely in her bed.
He kept his musings deep within.
But still it was, that he was led
to watch the elfin prince with closer eye.
And Ob'ron's training carried on
as 'Bekah grew before his face.
She learned of stars, and moon, and sun,
and what held heavens in their place
and on the power of magic did rely.

XXXVI

The girl now grew in loveliness
and left behind her frame of child
a woman now, and surely blessed
with sweetness in a spirit mild
and all Rebekah's beauty did revere.
Now Merlin trained her well in art
of magic craft and secret skill
and 'Bekah then did take the part
of righteousness, and by her will
and grace, the ways of justice did make clear.

XXXVII

But as she reached maturity
did Oberon upon her gaze
and female beauty did he see
that truly set his heart ablaze
and thus desired to have her for himself.
Then much attention did he pay,
desiring her within his heart.
He walked with her within the way
and of his passion made a start
to see if 'Bekah now could love an elf.

XXXVIII

Thus now that elf, he did begin
a declaration of his love
to make to 'Bekah. Deep within
his heart he wanted her to give
herself to him that he might her possess.
But 'Bekah's thoughts were not of such
for she her spirit had now set
and in her heart desired much
(and knew the longing would be met)
to take her place in works of righteousness.

XXXIX

She set her face to study hard
and of her books she made no end
and thus was always on her guard
but sought thus no one to offend
as she did now develop her own power.
No time had she for thoughts of love
but set herself exclusively
to learn the ways of powers above
determining full constantly
to walk her father's path now, hour by hour.

XL

Thus, when the elf confronted her
with declaration of his heart,
did she and Merlin now confer
since she did not want to be part
of cause of strife 'twixt men and elfin kind.
Then Merlin looked upon his child
and saw that she was now full-grown.
And in his image was she styled.
He saw now how the years had flown
and immaturity she'd left behind.

XLI

Thus, spake he unto 'Bekah mild,
"My daughter, 'twas my dearest thought
that thou, my one and only child,
would walk with me and evil thwart.
But if thou chooseth love, I understand.
For power of love is greater yet
than power of magic in the heart
but if thou lov'st, do not forget
that righteousness, it is thy part.
So tell me, will thou take this Ob'ron's hand?"

XLII

"Nay, father," now the girl replied.
"I make it full clear unto thee,
I never said, nor have implied
(and this is obvious to me)
unto the elf that I did harbour love
for him, nor yet for any man.
I stand alone unto this day,
and ever did since I begin
and chose to walk within in thy way
and set my mind on righteousness above."

XLIII

"Reject I now this outer world,
of love, and wealth, and empty praise.
For I would rather truth unfurl
and learn still more, my father's ways,
thy values to uphold with all my life.
But my concern I voice to thee,
is if I now reject the elf,
what consequences will there be?
For power he doth seek for himself
and he would surely have me as his wife."

XLIV

Then Merlin unto 'Bekah spake.
"My child, thou bringest to me joy
to know that thou wouldst seek to make
thy life a temple, and employ
thy powers in pursuit of righteous truth.
Go quickly now unto the elf
and speak to him in softest tone.
Tell him thou feel'st within thyself
thou canst not make with him thy home.
But see he does not think thee now aloof."

XLV

"And maybe he will see in thee
when looking on thine inward part
the power and nobility
that ever motivates thy heart
and understand that thou dost not him love.
'tis time that he return-ed home
and took his place in Elfindom
and leave thee to dwell here alone
till thine inheritance doth come
and thou dost take thy place as Albion's Judge."

XLVI

Then 'Bekah went unto the elf
and spake to him her father's word.
Then thought she now within herself
that as she was by him revered
he would her choice and circumstance respect.
But as she did communicate
she saw the anger in his eyes
and nothing would eradicate
the violence that in him did rise
– immediately his love he did forget.

XLVII

Rejection could not Ob'ron bear
or failure, or to feel a fool
and as he stood before her there
his heart to ice did surely cool.
Then looked he on her now most hatefully.
Controlled he yet his words and spake
a prophecy unto the maid;
said, "Madam, thou dost me forsake
and art the agent of my rage?
Thou shalt look on thy choice regretfully."

XLVIII

"For I shall make my task of life
whilst Merlin watches and will see
to pour within thy heart great strife,
eradicate his dynasty
and of great Albion make mere ashes now.
For thou and he abused full well
an elfin prince of strength and power
and I shall see thee yet in Hell
beware now of my vengeance hour.
So take my words to heart, thou batten cow."

XLIX

Then in a moment he was gone
and 'Bekah stood there all alone.
She felt the weight of Albion,
her father's joy, her only home.
Then wept she now, for prospect of revenge
might weigh upon her father's heart
and drive him to an early grave
though she did not eschew his part
and could, if called, dear Albion save:
she knew the elf would wounded pride avenge.

III

THE ENSLAVEMENT OF ELFINDOM

L

Thus Oberon to Elfindom
return-ed now with angry heart
and when to Mordain's court he'd come
did make his purpose from the start
to overthrow his father from the throne.
But when he first the King did see
great loyalty did Ob'ron feign
and prostrated himself, did he,
acknowledging the rightful reign
of Mordain, Captain-King of elves alone.

LI

But secretly, by dead of night
did Ob'ron gather unto him
an evil faction of great might
and in the dark he did begin
to plot how he would seize his father's power.
Then certain Elven knights he took,
and with the magic he did know
did Oberon begin to look
for perfect chance to overthrow
the rule of Mordain at the earliest hour.

LII

Now, Mordain dearly loved his son
and trusted him beyond reproach
so when advisers now did come
and sense of danger they did broach
the Captain-King would not believe a word.
"My son acknowledged that my reign
was righteous when he was returned
from Albion, and it is our gain
to utilise the truths he's learned
and all his wisdom, it is time we heard."

LIII

"Thus this decision I did take:
to elevate my only son
and Chancellor I shall him make
to rule all over Elfindom.
And he shall answer only unto me.
The kingdom thus shall benefit
from righteous works and magic power
and I shall in great comfort sit
as I begin my elder hour
and leisure shall I now begin to see."

LIV

The Elvin Nobles did confer
and saw the weakness of this case.
And they would ask him to defer
his policy and in its place
to set a council to assist the King.
But Mordain would have none of it
and angry did he then become:
"Dost thou not see the benefit?
To Elfindom I give my son
for by his hand the kingdom shall begin..."

LV

"...to be enhanced and prosper too
that I might take a little rest.
For soon my duties shall be through.
As Captain-King I think it best
to give my son a chance to learn my way
of ruling while I yet now live
that he might start to grow in grace.
Experience I shall him give
before by law he takes my place
and rules when I am dead as he will say."

LVI

The kingdom was disquieted much
for all did know well by repute
the fear that lay in Ob'ron's touch
and how he often did impute
disloyalty to those he did disdain.
Thus all in Elfindom did wait
with bated breath and heavy heart
to see if it was now too late
and whether he would evil start
when to the role of Chancellor he came.

LVII

The King determined to create
a ceremony in the court
and thus he would communicate
(of argument he would hear naught)
the day he would make Ob'ron Chancellor.
And when th' investiture was come
and all the nobles gathered there
the swearing, now it was begun.
Then deeply now did many fear
that Oberon would hunger even more…

LVIII

...for total power in Elfindom
to rule the kingdom in his way.
And many thought he had begun
to set his heart that very day
to separate King Mordain from his power.
And then the moment did arrive
to swear allegiance to the King
and Oberon, he did arise
but as his oath he did begin
commotion in the court did swiftly flower.

LIX

A batt'ring at the door was heard
it creaked and groaned and then caved in.
There entered in an elfin hoard
and with their swords they did begin
to take the lives of many in that place.
The royal guard, they did protect
King Mordain as he stood aghast.
The evil knights, they did select
as targets those that in the past
the cause of King and country did embrace.

LX

And thus the strongest in the court
and those who did revere the King
lost lives because of their support
and evil power did begin
to sway the battle under Mordain's gaze.
He call-ed to his only son
"Hail, Oberon – defend me now!
For thou art my dear chosen one
this evil must thou not allow!
Thy silence doth thy father now amaze!"

LXI

The court in bloody chaos stood,
and all around were bodies strewn.
And elves of evil and of good
lay lifeless where they had been hewn.
Then Ob'ron to his father slowly turned.
King Mordain at his son did stare
and speechless was he in that day
said not a word, but waited there
for explanation. Come what may
he loved his son – and thought his love returned.

LXII

"My royal father," he began,
"thou thought to see my power raise high
and over all of Elfindom
thou would have set me here today:
I thank thee for thy generosity.
It seems to me that such a gift
and all that thou for me hast done –
that thou didst make me long persist
to train and learn in Albion –
demands immediate reciprocity."

LXIII

Then Ob'ron lifted up his hand
and silently his lips did move
in invocation, and began
his full extent of power to prove
and under Mordain now the earth did break.
A pit did surely open now
and formed a gateway into Hell.
No mercy did he now allow
as he continued with his spell
and demons rose, the Captain-King to take.

LXIV

And Mordain still spake not a word
as evil demons round him flew
nor did he try to touch his sword
for his own fate he clearly knew.
But felt he sadness for his son that day.
And as he disappeared from view
great terror in the court did rise
for all did see that it was true
that Ob'ron's power and his lies
had given him the kingdom, come what may.

LXV

And thus it was that Oberon
with knights and with his magic power
did seize the throne of Elfindom
and straightway forward from that hour
did deepest terror settle on the good.
He ruled by evil and by might
and sought he ever to increase
his strength (not for the truth or right) –
and this deep hunger would not cease
whilst other kingdoms independent stood.

LXVI

And thus he turned his hungry eyes
to nearby lands possessed by man.
For humans did he deep despise
and hated all in Albion.
Nor would the other kingdoms now escape.
For acquisition did he seek
and dominance of all around
and deepest havoc would he wreak
till death and fear, they did abound.
Nor would he temper aught for pity's sake.

LXVII

But Oberon his time did bide.
As he amassed more pow'r and strength
his elfin armies did he hide
and sought to go to any length
to cover his intentions well from man.
But made he ready to invoke
the powers of Hell in his support
and sought he not now to provoke
responses from the human court
while all his preparations he began.

IV
THE APPOINTMENT OF HARMONY

LXVIII

And thus it was that happened there,
a golden age seemed ushered in
in Norsedane, eastern kingdom fair,
in Freedom, and in Albion.
And all the men of Gaia dwelt in peace.
Their trade and culture did enhance
and life was good within their shores.
But if there should arise, perchance,
disputes, or actions without cause
the Judges made sure evilness did cease.

LXIX

But thus in Merlin's middle age
a delegation did arrive
from Freedom, to consult the Sage
and from his wisdom to derive
some benefit to suit the kingdoms three.
A Judge was out of Freedom sent,
to meet with Merlin, Judge to Judge;
(in this pursuit would not relent)
for spirits moved them from above
and thus they sent to him Judge Harmony.

LXX

And she would now a Wittan make,
a conference of kingdoms three.
In Norsedane, Vidar, he had spake,
and he with Harmony did agree –
that human kingdoms must themselves defend
'gainst elfin hoards that now did mass
themselves and gather up for war.
And what he feared would come to pass
was Oberon would hunger more
and unto thoughts of war would he then tend.

LXXI

And thus, the Wittan now was set
for coming spring in Freedom's land.
But Merlin did with deep regret
decline the offer, but would send
his daughter, 'Bekah, as his alternate.
For care had he of Albion
and wanted all men there to see
the love he held for his dear home
and how responsibility
he took for cares of men and cares of state.

LXXII

Thus spoke he unto 'Bekah fair,
and told her that his heart would break
if aught befell her journey there
and thus was minded so to make
request of Harmony to take her home.
Thus Harmony and her entourage
departed then from Albion's shore,
took fair Rebekah in her charge
and set her face for home once more
and she true friends with 'Bekah did become.

LXXIII

For as they voyaged 'cross the sea
and weeks of hardship did endure,
the girl did seek her company
and came to love her all the more
despite the fact that Harmony age-d was.
Thus 'Bekah sought to learn of her
and sat she at the elder's feet
and made it plain she did prefer
her over others she did meet.
For growth of learning did she make her cause.

LXXIV

Thus, when they sighted Freedom's land
And Harmony's heart within her leapt
she took Rebekah by the hand
and would not let her go except
the girl agreed to sojourn at her home.
So Harmony did take her in
and she did there the winter spend
and so the elder did begin
to see the girl as dearest friend.
Thus Harmony no longer dwelt alone.

LXXV

More like a daughter, treated she
Rebekah whilst she there did stay
and deep fulfilled was Harmony
and often of the girl did pray
that she would now of Freedom make her home.
Now 'Bekah truly torn-ed was,
for she did not this love begrudge;
but loved her father, and because
she set her heart to be a Judge
determined she must needs return alone...

LXXVI

...to Albion when all was done
and when the Wittan was complete
and when the Norseman too was come
she planned that she would him entreat
to see her home for her dear father's sake.
But Harmony sought to persuade
Rebekah now to tarry there
She thought that she could her dissuade
and make her from her choice forbear.
So thus to her a promise she did make.

LXXVII

For Harmony knew that her age
would soon prevent her to discharge
her duties, and though yet a Sage,
she soon would not remain a Judge
and Freedom a replacement would appoint.
But she would argue 'Bekah's cause
and see her now a Judge become,
and thought this was a gain, because
it made a link with Albion.
She thought that other Judges would anoint...

LXXIII

...Rebekah as a Judge that year
to seal now their relationship
with Merlin's court and make full clear
that they did make a partnership
that Oberon would have to treat with care.
And thus, when winter's end drew nigh
and spring began her head to raise
did Freedom lift its heart and cry
unto the gods and made full praise
that now a new Judge was appointed there.

LXXIX

And when th' anointing day was come
and all the court did gather round
did Harmony stand, her work near done
with 'Bekah, who, in thought profound
did contemplate within herself her oath.
Then Harmony did her anoint
with oil upon her flaxen hair
and with this action did appoint
Rebekah as a Judge, full clear.
And then Rebekah to the Judges quoth:

LXXX

"I am true blessed by thee today
and rise will I, unto this task.
For I will serve now, come what may,
the land of Freedom, and will ask
for nothing in return. For I shall be
full satisfied if I may bring
more love and peace unto this land.
And if I do, my heart will sing.
And for this cause now understand
that I do take the title 'Harmony'."

LXXXI

"For to her wisdom I aspire
and if I can walk in her way
perhaps her grace I shall acquire
and be to thee in coming day
a shadow of my mentor's probity.
The name Rebekah I will yield,
for though it is my name of choice,
with this appointment I am sealed
unto the task. And thus my voice
shall answer now when call-ed "Harmony."

LXXXII

The Judges then did her embrace
and their approval signify
by sitting her within her place
and with this act did dignify
the office of the Judge that she did hold.
And ever forth would she been known
as Harmony, and by that name
Rebekah hoped that she had shown
that she would serve not power and fame,
but in the cause of righteousness be bold.

V

THE COMING OF THE NORSEMAN

LXXXIII

And now the winter was full past,
and sun was stronger in the sky,
then did Vidar come at last
and to the Wittan would apply
his strength, attention and vitality.
And thus were all the nations come
to conference in the common cause.
And great debate, it was begun,
intensively and without pause
to serve the needs of all humanity.

LXXXIV

Now, Vidar was a mighty man,
of stature great, and powerful heart.
And when he spoke and thus began
with dignity now to impart
his wisdom unto all assembled there,
then did Harmony look on him
and for his grace had deep respect
and it was then she did begin
her chosen course now to regret.
Here stood a man for whom she could well care.

LXXXV

For many suitors had pursued
her while she was in former life
when thoughts of learning did preclude
all wish of hers to be a wife –
for none had passed her way that she could love.
But here before her stood a man
who loved the truth as much she.
And thus it was, she now began
to wish that she was truly free.
But still she could not of this course approve.

LXXXVI

Thus, when the Wittan was recessed
did Harmony now Vidar seek
for in herself was sore distressed
and unto him she now would speak –
that she would not the conference compromise.
She planned to tell him to his face
She was distracted full, in truth
though in his heart she sought no place
but hoped he would not hold reproof
or even worse, her feelings now despise.

LXXXVII

She in the garden him did spy,
Intending him now to approach;
but could not on herself rely
with stable voice this now to broach:
the subject that she wished to raise with him.
So when she did now him confront
expected she that they would speak
of forming now a common front
'gainst Oberon as he did seek
his evil works in Gaia to begin.

LXXXVIII

But when she did look in his eyes
great softness there did she perceive
and all at once did realise
in Vidar's heart there now did live
true warmth for her that she'd reciprocate.
And for his part he too did see
that she did hold him in her heart
and that she now would seek to be
partaker of a better part
then merely to with him participate...

LXXXIX

…in Wittan and alliances
and matters made in politics,
in issues made in conferences,
and means to counter elfin tricks –
for he her love did see within her eyes.
And at that moment Vidar knew
his love for her she did return
and it was not hid from his view
nor thought he now this love to spurn.
But neither could begin to compromise…

XC

…th' affairs of nations, or of man
as all did stand in common cause
since Oberon had now begun
to test their limits without pause.
And thus these two were troubled by their heart.
And so it was, they did agree
they must postpone their happiness
and both would have to wait to be
together, and would not confess
to others that they chose now not to part.

XCI

But day by day their love did grow,
and Harmony deep troubled was.
For Vidar soon would have to go
to Norsedane, where he was a Judge
and she must now remain in Freedom's part.
Though her responsibility
would Harmony not compromise,
for her own part she'd rather be
possessor of a lover's prize
and hold her Vidar close unto her heart.

XCII

And as the time did pass away,
and days were spent in conference,
did neither of the two delay
when chance arose, to hurry thence
unto a secret place they did agree.
And there they would their love declare
and in each other take delight.
For though they were both full aware
that other circumstances might
cause parting of the ways they both did see…

XCIII

...that each did need the other's touch.
And they would take what time they could
and both did feel that for as much
as was within them, thus they would
together be, and join their hearts as one.
So deep did their commitment reach
that they were married in the heart
though each the other did beseech
not to forget that they must part –
for days of conference were nearly done.

VI

VIOLATION

XCIV

And as the Wittan did proceed
the spies of Oberon were rife
for he did clearly see a need
to cause twixt humans greatest strife,
and thus their planned alliance to destroy.
But it did great frustrate the elf
who wanted now his chance to see
to take more strength unto himself
at every opportunity
by all and every means he could employ...

XCV

...that when the spies reported back
intelligence from Freedom's court,
that there was not a single crack
in the alliance that they wrought
and all the humans spoke with single voice.
For peace in Gaia did they seek
and all aggression would withstand.
They knew that Ob'ron sought to wreak
great havoc in the heart of man.
To stand together – this was now their choice.

XCVI

And then it came to pass one day
as Ob'ron's spy did walk abroad
that he did pass a different way
and chanced to hear a single word
of Vidar's voice as he to Harmony spoke.
Regrettably, that word was "love"
which stopped the elf spy in his way.
Then he did climb a tree above
the place where they did spend that day
and thus their secrets did he now uncloak.

XCVII

And he did watch the two embrace
as each did love to lover show
as all alone in secret place
they thought themselves to be, and now
deep passion of the hearts did demonstrate.
And thus the elf spy did perceive
a chance to gain the upper hand
as they love's hunger did relieve
did he return unto his band
and all that he had seen he did relate.

XCVIII

Now when the news to Ob'ron came
he saw his opportunity
For though he thought all love inane
a perfect chance he now did see:
asunder would he split the hearts of men.
An evil plan he now did form
to set them at each other's throat
and brothers would apart be torn
as havoc he did now promote.
And also would he have revenge again.

XCIX

For long he had his anger held
'gainst Merlin and this 'Harmony',
and hatred in his heart had dwelled.
But now he did perceive the key
for recompense, that they did once disdain
and mock him in his foolishness.
For now he had outgrown his youth
and sought for only one caress;
one lover and, it was in truth,
the love of human death and human pain.

C

And he could scarce contain his joy
but knew he must compose himself.
He subterfuge would now employ,
and pose as human, not as elf,
and thus be seen as man of Albion.
He then a schism would create
when he did execute his plan
and deepest evil perpetrate
to terrify the heart of man –
then revel in the chaos that would come.

CI

Three trusted spies he took with him
and they from Albion seemed to be.
Then readied he to make his sin
and take revenge on Harmony.
Thus, waited they at Vidar's trysting place.
And then, as evening did approach
and Harmony would Vidar meet,
she thought the subject now to broach
and would her lover now entreat
to stay in Freedom, and there to embrace…

CII

...her as his wife and find a way
to govern Norsedane from that place
– in any case, with her to stay
(she thought that she could make a case
and thus persuade him to remain with her).
But when she came where they would meet
the elves sprang forth as men of war.
As if from Albion they did greet
her and declare they'd come from far
at Merlin's word, and with him did concur...

CIII

...that Vidar was with elves in league
and sought the Wittan to destroy
and on his promise would renege
and that his love was just a ploy
to lull her into false security.
But when she did objection make
they held her fast and tied her down
and sought her righteousness to take
and make her outcast by renown –
and violate her virtue bodily.

CIV

Then as they had their evil way
did Vidar happen on the scene.
For something caused him short delay
but rushed he at his lover's scream
and maddened was he at what he did see.
Then drew he forth his sword at once
and sought his lover to defend
and would her violators trounce,
protect his lover and them send
to Hell where they quite clear deserved to be.

CV

But four were just beyond his strength
and they his sword did take away.
They violated her at length
as they did Vidar hold at bay,
and forced his eyes to watch the evil scene.
Thus, violent anger in him rose
as he did contemplate this harm
and if he could, he would have chose
to sacrifice himself, and calm
would be to give his life to save her there.

CVI

But when they now were done with her
and scarce in consciousness was she
they did amongst themselves confer
and ti-ed her unto the tree –
that she her lover's death would contemplate.
And him they bound to horses three,
by arms and legs, and did create
disturbance, and set horses free.
And thus his body they did break.
And Harmony was forced to watch his fate.

CVII

Then made they clear a second time
their origin was Albion
and they had come at Merlin's sign
and his command, and all was done
because he wanted 'Bekah to protect.
But Harmony was close to death
or close to madness, true to say.
She thought to take a final breath
and to her lover go that day.
Thus, ending of her life she did expect.

CVIII

But her tormentors set her free
and cut the ropes that held her fast.
Unbound her, did they, from the tree.
She sank upon the ground at last
and lay in utter, silent misery.
When elves were gone she did begin
to drag herself to Vidar's frame;
held fast to what was left of him
and softly she did speak his name
and him did cradle underneath the tree…

CIX

…where they their love had often made;
where looked they in each other's eyes;
where they their lovers' games had played;
where they had come to realise
that each without the other could not live.
There she did hold him close to her
where once he oft her name would say;
or sometimes silence did prefer
as hand-in-hand they spent the day.
Now all these precious times she did relive.

CX

She sat with him throughout the night
and would not cease his name to speak
and when the day did dawn full bright
no other purpose did she seek
than to caress him 'til her death would be.
But noticed was her absence now,
and many came to seek for her.
Then found they her beneath the bough
and in one thought they did concur:
that madness overtook now Harmony.

CXI

Thus gently did they lift her up.
But she would not her lover leave.
Unto her lips they pressed a cup
of wine, as if her strength to give
then gently led her, sobbing, from that place.
Then upright men did Vidar take
and placed they him into a grave.
And they did hold a funeral wake
and so his mem'ry sought to save.
For Vidar was a man of noble grace.

CXII

But Harmony they did remove
and in her bed they plac-ed her.
But yet she called out for her love
and sobbed so deep they did concur
in this: that she might never now return
from place of madness in her mind
where she did lie by day and night.
For she to reason now was blind
and seemed to have no moral sight
but ever did she for her Vidar yearn.

CXIII

And she then by his grave would sit
And stay with him all through the night.
Her thoughts to him she did remit
and talked to him, and thought it right
to take her life to be with him again.
And all that did prevent her now
was that she unto Hell might go
while Vidar was in Heav'n, and how
she would not then his presence know,
by reason of a grievous mortal sin.

CXIV

With Vidar's death the Wittan came
abruptly to an end that day.
And all the delegates felt shame
was done to Norsedane, and did say
that the alliance now could not proceed.
And thus, they to their various parts
returned with heavy heads held low,
and deepest sadness in their hearts,
for each within themselves did know
that no one had the skills to intercede…

CXV

…amongst the numerous interests there
in quite the way that Vidar had.
For to him, all their hearts did bare
and Norsedane wisdom made them glad.
But now the mighty man of peace was gone.
And all did hold unspoken fear:
without a leader to unite
all nations and declare it clear
that they would for true justice fight,
a greater power would come to Oberon.

VII

DRAGONSONG

CXVI

For six long months did Harmony lie
and only on the wall did gaze
and hoped she constantly to die
but only this thought did her save:
to bring her Vidar's killers to the light.
For mercy then did she beseech
the gods, and prayed that they would bring
true justice now within her reach
so that at least she could begin
to set her lover's murder to the right.

CXVII

We gods were silent at her call.
But though she once did truth embrace,
it was while she did face the wall
a newer thought her mind did trace:
that righteousness forsook her on that day.
And thus her heart to anger turned
and madness did distil to rage
and for revenge she did deep yearn
and nothing would this thirst assuage
for she would have his killers, come what may.

CXVIII

So after months of deepest pain
her anger burned within her well
and if the gods would her disdain
then she would turn for help to Hell
and with the demons now a bargain make.
Thus called she on the darkest power
to energise her in that place
and give her demon strength that hour
and show to her the murderers' face
and for this vengeance, Hell her soul would take.

CXIX

The King of demons came to her
that night, and would the bargain seal.
He did with her now long confer,
that if she sold herself to Hell
then dragon power would be her prize that day.
By madness was her heart now turned
and she this bargain did accept.
For vengeance sweet she truly yearned
and in herself could not reject
the chance her lover's killers to repay.

CXX

So when the deed in blood was sealed,
the demon did depart from her
and magic was to her revealed
and in the sin she did concur;
that she her soul did sell to Hell for might.
When all was quiet in that place
a power came upon her frame
contorted now became her face
as she a dragon did become
and dragonsong roared forth into the night.

CXXI

She screamed her agony at last
as voice she found and pain declared
for all the evil that was passed
and all the suff'ring she had shared.
Then Harmony exuded hate that hour.
Thus energised by deepest pain
she rose in strength into the night
and life would never be the same
as dragon thus did take to flight
and on the land it flaunted now its power.

CXXII

Possessed with single thought was she:
true recompense in Albion.
She sought to have and thus to be
reveng-ed for the only man
that she had loved in all her days now gone.
Possessed by madness she did fly
across the sea to Albion's shore
with purpose simply to make die
her lover's killers, and still more –
her vengeance to inflict on Albion.

CXXIII

And as she flew along the shore
by madness still was she possessed.
Her anger boiled within her more
and it must also be confessed,
that she no longer cared whom she would kill.
On death her mind was focused now
and she destruction sought to bring
and given the chance, would full allow
her dragonsong to fully sing
and bring to Albion hearts the deepest chill...

CXXIV

...of death as she her rage did free
and give full vent to all her pain
and havoc would wreak constantly
and kill, and kill, and kill again.
And now at last a target she did spy:
a little village by the coast
where only honest men did dwell
– two hundred souls at very most –
and these she sought to send to Hell
her deepest urge to kill could not deny.

CXXV

Now once she had the taste of blood
there simply was no stopping her.
And there was just no power of god
or man that could her rage defer
and village after village she did burn.
A trail of desolation lay
behind her as she came to Court
of Albion, for to Merlin slay
for he, as architect, had wrought
the death of Vidar, and he soon would learn...

CXXVI

...the touch of dragon lips upon
his furrowed brow and on his heart
and he would hear the dragonsong
and would repaid be for his part
in Vidar's death – or so she did surmise.
And thus she now returned to ground
and onto Gaia placed her claws
and in that place made not a sound
nor did she make a single pause
as she her aim did seek to realise.

CXXVII

But as she entered in the Court
did Merlin stand in front of her
and mighty magic now was wrought
but still he would with her confer
if she would only listen to his case.
Now well beyond the reach was she
of reason or of human voice
and Merlin now could clearly see
that he was left with little choice
but her to banish far from human face.

CXXVIII

In agony he lifted up
his hands unto the heavens high
his tears did roll – he wished this cup,
he sorely wished, would pass him by.
But only by one act could he redeem
the evil that had now been wrought
so far abroad in Albion.
Thus, spell he did cast in that court
and summoned demons now to come
to take his daughter from the place she'd been…

CXXIX

…brought up and taught the ways of truth;
where she her training did commence;
where she had spent her girlish youth;
where she had learned her adult sense.
From here would Harmony be banished now,
unto the deepest part of Hell
and there her sin to contemplate.
Then on her did he cast his spell
and all his pow'r did concentrate.
Thus unto Hell he did the dragon show.

CXXX

Then silently the demons came
and took the dragon by the wing
and stop-ed they the powerful flame
and slowly did they now begin
within the bowels of Gaia to descend.
But Merlin stood in anguish now –
knew not how such could come to be
and how it was he did allow
the elf to cause such misery
for all this evil did on him depend.

CXXXI

The Judge now full exhausted was,
enthusiasm could he not
find in himself for other cause
nor did he care a single jot
for any other issue than this pain.
His child he had now sent to Hell.
Her lover died a fearful death.
And thousands, did he know full well,
because of her did draw last breath
and Albion would never be the same.

CXXXII

And thus it was he did decide
the Judgeship to relinquish now
and in another would confide
and make a king to rule below
while he did go to live on astral plane.
Thus Arthur did he now appoint
to rule the kingdom in his stead
and as the king did now anoint,
and with his wisdom Arthur fed,
for cares of state were on him deepest drain.

EPILOGUE

CXXXIII

The wing-ed god his head did bow,
as he did near the end of tale.
In detail had he told me now
and exposition left him frail
– if frail a god could ever really be.
And thus he looked me in the eye
to see if I reaction made
or if I now away would fly
or would my promise now evade.
Thus my response he seemed to seek of me.

CXXXIV

So thus I spake now unto him,
"Great Mercury, I do perceive
or think I now I do begin
to understand why thou dost grieve
for dragonsong from Hell let loose again.
But still I wish to understand
why life of man has been cut short
and why it is that human span
is not as long as thou hast taught
but now is merely threescore years and ten."

CXXXV

"Dear Scribe," he did reply to me,
"in all my words hast thou not known
if thou a friend of Hell would be
a seed of death, it must be sown.
For now I tell thee true, for thou wouldst know:
that to relieve the human race
of dragonsong, did Merlin make
a bargain deep within that place
where demons did his daughter take
and this was his agreement there below:"

CXXXVI

"If Hell would bind the dragon fast
and hold her for eternity
the lives of men would end at last
when all did reach to seventy.
This was the price that Merlin had to pay
to rid the world of Harmony,
his daughter whom he loved so well.
And she would ever now bound be
in deepest chasms down in Hell
and never will his torment flee away."

CXXXVII

"And thus it is gods cannot make
determination in this cause.
For moral right did Merlin take
upon himself, and this because
it was the only way to free your race.
And so we have concluded now
that it must take another man
a moral choice to make below
and end the story now begun.
Thus, this decision's set before thy face."

CXXXVIII

"And now, good Scribe, 'tis time for me
to take my leave and from thee part.
Thus all alone thou now must be
and full consider in the heart
the outcome that in Gaia now shall be.
Consider well and carefully.
Weigh all the issues in thy mind.
Attendant to thy duty be,
that all the world might surely find
true honour in thine own morality."

CXXXIX

Then with these final words he left
and I was once again alone.
Of all support I was bereft
and Counsellors, I had not one,
as I did take responsibility.
And thus again I must take up
my quill and write another book.
And I shall drink now of this cup,
and in my own heart I shall look,
when I next tell my story unto thee.

CXL

For at that time, 'twill be the case
that I shall write in prophecy.
The future of the human race
and individuals shall be
within my hands – and I want not this pow'r.
An arbiter I have been made
of moral choice for human kind
and thus I cannot now evade
determination in my mind.
I must address this choice within the hour.

BOOK THE FOURTH

THE SLEEP STONE

PROLOGUE

I

Full seven nights and seven days
have passed since Mercury came to me
and still 'tis hard the strength to raise
to take my quill in prophecy
and speak a moral ending to this tale.
For given the choice I would then see
great happiness come unto all
– for Vidar to rise bodily
– for Michael to fall in a thrall
and good o'er evil truly to prevail.

II

Each night I set me to the task
and verses pen that please my eye
but always do I have to ask
for on me now the gods rely
– is this a moral ending that I write?
And when my work I contemplate
that righteousness is full restored,
that truth from lies doth emanate
and peace it reigneth all abroad –
then inspiration from me doth take flight.

III

Now I must write in congruence
and tell thee what is in my heart
for Gaia do I influence
and must thus take an honest part
in setting out the future that will be.
For gods will not be fooled, mark you!
True moral choice they do require.
Reality must now accrue
and not some puff of weak desire.
Solutions to dilemmas would they seek.

IV

A mortal's choice, then, shall I make
as I set forth most solemnly
and shall not truth incarcerate
but grant unto it liberty.
And thus, it shall the tale's end now define.
So suffering must play its part
and sorrow I expect to see
for now 'tis time to make a start,
to re-establish history
– emotion and morality assign.

V

Why does this task fall unto me?
And who am I to make such choice?
I agonise now constantly
and shrink from lifting up my voice.
No man should such task be thus assigned!
The gods, they think they honour me
– pay homage to my eloquence.
But I would from this be set free
and agonise for recompense.
Yet I am chosen by them to remind...

VI

...humanity and Elfindom
no step is without consequence
and acts which we have once begun
to take without a just defence
will surely one day unto us return.
So mark you well, thou mortal soul
that all our acts discover us!
And if thou wouldst now be made whole
remember, life is tenuous.
Consider all this well and thou shalt learn.

ꝉ
THE SEER RETURNS

VII

She stood upon the astral plane
with clench-ed fists and facing sky.
Her tears did flow like falling rain
and emanated thus a cry:
"Why hath my love from me been taken now?"
A body lay before her feet
and moving not, it was quite still.
With sorrow was her heart replete
and even thoughts of dragon-kill
no sense of satisfaction did allow.

VIII

Thus, Attie bared her soul full well
and heaven did gaze on her pain.
At last, she understood the spell
that did ensure she would remain
in solitude, for joy had not her found.
And nothing could her compensate
for loss of love that she held dear.
No storyteller could relate
the way she did her love revere
who lay before her, silent, on the ground.

IX

Her heart was screaming now, in pain.
Her agony it did abound.
For soon she had to go again
and set her feet upon the ground
of Freedom, where she did her life begin.
But still she could not her remove
as sorrow unto sorrows cried
and still she yearn-ed for her love
and wish that she herself had died
and mystified was she as to her sin.

X

For she did only ever serve
the truth, and cleave to righteousness –
did nothing for herself reserve
and always did her heart confess
so why should she be treated in this way?
She asked for little – only love
and to be with her heart's desire
for whom she did now rise above
to astral plane, and did not tire
his interests to pursue there day-to-day.

XI

And when the truth was full revealed
and full unmasked was Harmony
she had thought then that he would yield
and let her love him constantly.
Yet now his empty shell before her lay.
And weeping both from heart and eyes
she lifted him into her arm,
(his mortal frame did not despise)
she bore him up, so strangely calm,
and silently did rise and steal away.

XII

She thus unto the lake did come
where she her childhood days had spent
and placed him in her cabin home
and of her love could not repent.
She lay him down still silent on her bed.
Then gazed she on his ashen face
and heard his voice within her heart.
Of life she saw there was no trace
and sure was she his soul did part
and that her lover, Michael, was full dead.

XIII

Then sound at door disturb-ed her
but she resented company.
She thought an answer to defer
for all alone she wished to be,
to grieve at will for Michael who was gone.
But knock at door persisted now
and she was forced to answer it.
Before her stood – she knew not how –
the beggar, and she did permit
his entry once again into her home.

XIV

The beggar took her unto him
and silently her tears did flow.
In gentlest terms he did begin
to tell her what she must now know:
the history that we did here relate.
Thus softly spake he unto her
and talked to her all through the night.
And she did let herself defer
to gentleness so that she might
give no more thought to what would be her fate.

XV

He talked on as the sun did rise
and not a word did he withhold.
She honesty did not despise
and knew it was the truth he told.
So now she knew the story from the start.
But as he did near the story's end
these words he did speak unto her,
"Dear Attie, dost thou comprehend
and art thou ready to concur
these issues are much bigger than thy heart?"

XVI

"For all our futures do rely
and even man's continuance
on what now happens, by the by,
and greatly on our providence
in action we take for humanity.
Now, shortly I must ask of thee
an act of greatest sacrifice.
In mortal danger thou must be
and often act without advice
– I ask thee to fulfil a prophecy."

XVII

"And if thou dost this task accept
then many turmoils wilt thou face
and many dangers must deflect
and now must save the human race
and Elfindom from dragonsong once more.
Two truths I now speak unto thee:
the first, thy Michael is not dead,
but waiting is he, patiently,
and thinks his soul will soon be led
by angels shortly unto heaven's shore."

XVIII

"But he is in the Place of Trance
and still he has the choice to make
– accepting heaven's circumstance
or yet more mortal life to take.
But still his heart doth yearn for Harmony.
But now he's seen her evilness
he sees no point in living on
and spending years in deep distress
and thus would rather now be drawn
to heaven where his soul will be set free."

XIX

"But I can still speak unto him
and influence the choice e'en now,
and with my energy begin
to draw him back and show him how
he too, his contribution now must make,
to saving man from dragonsong
before he thus can take his leave.
For though his choice is to be gone
this other service will he give
before his final exit he will take."

XX

"The second truth I also say
— that thou the dragon hast not slain,
nor dragonsong did take away
when thou didst go to astral plane
— for she partakes of immortality.
And if thou dost her heads remove
then she will simply grow yet more
and thus repeatedly will prove
the tales thou know'st from dragon lore
— that dragons live for all eternity."

XXI

Now all this while was Attie still
and looked at him with tear-stained face.
She sought the truth now to distil
and understand her personal place
in the unfolding web of history.
And it was hard for her to know
that yet more trials would come her way ·
and that her love did wish to go
to heaven and not with her stay
and that again her life was solit'ry.

XXII

But Merlin then spake once again,
"Dear Attie, now the time has come
for me to touch thy Michael's frame
so that the process is begun
of restoration of his soul from Trance."
Thus Merlin stood before the bed
and took the hands of his dear son.
He placed a kiss upon his head
and thus the magic was begun.
And slowly, surely, did it now advance.

XXIII

The purest light did fill that place
as energy did surely pass
from Merlin, who himself did brace,
to Michael, who did come at last
back to his body from the Place of Trance.
But Merlin's life force did deplete
and from exhaustion now he fell.
For thus the process did complete
and Attie there could surely tell
he did the cause of righteousness advance.

XXIV

From Michael's lips there came a sound
of steady breathing on the bed.
Now Merlin lay upon the ground.
For though the wizard was not dead,
he wearied from the loss of energy.
Then Attie wept, her love to see
as he returned unto his frame.
She knew that she herself was free
a little more time now to claim
and with her lover once again to be.

XXV

She sat beside him on the bed
and smiled to see his open eyes;
to know that he was not now dead
and mortal life did not despise,
but now return ed was he once again.
Then she remembered Merlin, too.
Concern-ed was she for his pain
as he did rouse himself anew
and rose to standing once again.
For she could see that he was not the same.

XXVI

Sore weakened was he from the act
of transference of energy
and she could see this for a fact:
that full depleted now was he –
exhaustion showed upon his age-ed face.
'Twas just as if more years had come
and added them to Merlin's age
and that his greatest work was done –
exhausted surely was the Sage,
and soon would he remove to heaven's grace.

II

THE BARGAIN MADE BEFORE THE DAWN OF TIME

XXVII

Now Michael rose him on the bed
and asked for water for his thirst.
Though now of death he had no dread
but knew that work he must do first,
before he could remove to heaven's gate.
"My children," spake the wizard now,
"my time on Gaia – it is short
but falls it to us now, somehow,
to save not just Arthurian court
but all of Gaia from a heinous fate."

XXVIII

"For dragonsong doth still resound.
And Michael, be thou now aware,
the dragon lover thou hast found –
she is my daughter, 'Bekah fair,
who for her madness dragon form did take."
And then he told the tale again
of how his daughter lost her mind
how righteousness forsook, and then
she lost her care for humankind
and how this sadness still his heart did break.

XXIX

"Judge not her harsh," he said to them,
"She suffered pain beyond compare.
Her human part would wish again
for righteousness, but doth despair
for dragon thoughts do oft her overtake.
And she, in error, hates me well
and I cannot reach unto her,
her heart is still caught in the spell
and will not to my love defer
and I cannot the evil spell now break."

XXX

"Now this I fear within my heart:
that Oberon will bend her will.
She still knows not that from the start
'twas he who did her lover kill.
Now he will surely seek to use her power.
And thus it falls now unto us
to rid the world of dragonsong,
and Elfindom free from the curse
and evil power of Oberon.
We to this task must set ourselves this hour."

XXXI

Then up spake Attie unto him,
"How can we quell this dragonsong
if I cannot e'en now begin
to slay the beast and see it gone?
Eternal life the creature doth partake."
Spake Merlin, "Thou art right, my dear.
The dragon lives eternally,
and in her heart she shows no fear
of death, but liveth constantly.
Do not her power underestimate."

XXXII

"Thus I shall tell thee now, my child,
though dragons cannot die, they sleep.
And though from disposition wild
their wakefulness they often keep,
'tis possible to sleep eternally.
But she cannot be forc-ed so,
and willingly must acquiesce
thus choosing unto sleep to go,
and then forsake unrighteousness
and so from all her pain she would be free."

XXXIII

"But sleep will not come easily
for wracked with terrors is she now
and memories come constantly
that she did Vidar's death allow
and thus she does for this seek to atone.
There is but one way she will sleep
and rest herself eternally
and thus once more her peace will keep
restoring Gaia constantly:
we must bring unto Harmony, the Stone."

XXXIV

"The Stone of Sleep – The Amulet –
its story I must now thee tell.
If she wears this she will forget
the terrors of her person'l Hell
and ever then partake of sleep sublime.
The Stone is buried deep within
the frozen wastes of Elfindom.
It lay there since time did begin
for reason that a deal was done –
a bargain made before the dawn of time."

XXXV

"The world was form-ed in six days
by God the Father far above.
Then Asgard made He for His praise
and separated, for His love
the place of demons, Hell, full deep below.
The gods of Asgard did he task
and gave responsibility.
For one great service did he ask
that they keep Gaia fully free
of demons and the hate that they would show."

XXXVI

"The gods did then negotiate
with Demon King from Hell below
that he would be full satiate
with Hell, and not to Gaia go
and thus were many demons put to sleep.
Two-thirds of all their number slept
– a demon army slumbering still.
And by the Sleep Stone are they kept
within the frozen Elfish hills.
And still the gods and demons this trust keep."

XXXVII

"The Sleep Stone is protected well
by Lord of Fire and Lord of Ice.
For thus it is the gods do quell
the demons, or must pay the price
of hell let loose upon dear Gaia's face.
The Sleep Stone holds the Gate to Hell
and keeps the demon army safe.
Now hear me clearly, know full well,
if set free, they will Gaia strafe
eradicating humans from this place."

XXXVIII

"Thus a dilemma do we face:
Removal of the dragonsong
may set the demons in this place
of Gaia where they then would long
make terror reign on lives of elves and men.
But Harmony must surely sleep
or dragon fire will many burn.
In trance she must be buried deep
and in this way her heart will turn
and Gaia will be freed from such again."

XXXIX

"Thus now this task you both must face:
to source the Stone in Elfindom
and bring it back unto this place.
We have one cycle of the sun
And thus for no more time can it be gone.
And in that time then Harmony
must choose to sleep of her own will
or wakened will the demons be
and all humanity will kill –
a terror greater still than dragonsong."

XL

"You have one month to find the Stone
– one single cycle of the moon.
This task you two must face alone.
You must not now return too soon
for one month hence we shall in this place meet.
And I shall bring the dragon here
and see if she will acquiesce.
Then shall we make our purpose clear
to her and hope she will confess
herself now ready for eternal sleep."

XLI

"Then in the cycle of the sun
she and the Stone must be returned
to Elfindom or else will come
the demon army as you learned
to spread destruction wide with evil pow'r.
So rise to meet thy destiny
and unto this, the single most
important challenge thou shalt see
or Gaia surely shall be lost!
Rise, Michael! Attie! 'Tis thy finest hour!"

XLII

Then Attie and the Seer rose,
prepar-ed they themselves to leave.
But Merlin, then he also chose
to take a moment now to grieve
for daughter 'Bekah, lost to dragon mind.
For pain he carried deep within
and felt himself to be the cause
of how the turmoil did begin
and then continued without pause
and realised that he no peace would find...

XLIII

...till he had put the wrongs to right
and made the world a peaceful place.
Though waning now his magic might
(though not his righteousness and grace)
he knew not if this task he could fulfil.
For now it fell unto his hand
to meet the dragon face-to-face
to see if she could understand
that evil did not have a place
and that the end of life was not to kill...

XLIV

...but to revive and energise
and live as one in bless-ed peace.
But would she now this truth despise
or would she yearn for sweet release
from turmoil? Did she still possess her soul?
No other way was there to know
but to confront her in her lair.
So unto astral plane he'd go
and stand before her without fear
and offer her the chance to be made whole.

XLV

But Merlin now felt very old
and weariness was on his heart.
His love for 'Bekah did he hold
and reticent to make a start
was he to bring her to eternal sleep.
Then opened he his heart and wept –
for child so lost to evilness.
And all his magic had not kept
her safe, as Nanna did profess
in Asgard when she him did warn to keep…

XLVI

…Rebekah safe from Oberon
protecting her from grievous harm
and he knew he had failed her long
and she was not a soothing balm
but cause of deep vexation to his soul.
Such bitter tears he now did shed
and fell they, caustic, on his heart.
And thus he did himself wish dead
– for death would be better part.
And nothing now could ever make her whole.

XLVII

He wept to moon and stars and sun
he screamed at Heaven deepest pain.
And thus his tears, now once begun
in mighty rivers thus they came
as he did cry a parent's deepest fears.
"My child! My child! Where hast thou gone?
And why art thou now lost to me?
Such hopes I had, my dearest one.
So much I wanted to give thee –
but evilness doth consummate thy years!"

XLVIII

Then fell he down upon his face
and beat the ground till earth did shake.
Yet thought it still a better place
than other paths he soon must take,
to give his daughter up unto her sleep.
But knew he this: she did forsake
all hope of full redemption now
and if she did remain awake
'twas obvious – he did see how –
all Gaia would be placed in terror deep.

XLIX

Thus Merlin knew what he must do,
and rose he up to stand again.
Now energy he had anew
to start the process once again
of separating dragon from her bower.
And put behind him, he, his pain
and set himself to task in hand,
and turned to matters once again
of bringing peace unto the land
and ending dragonsong and dragon power.

L

Then all removed them from that place
with Merlin bound for astral plane.
Thus Attie and the Seer would face
deep hardship as they sought again
to find the means to silence dragonsong.
Once more the cabin quiet was
and winter sun smiled on the lake
as all did now a righteous cause
pursue, and would of grace partake.
Now they their final journeys had begun.

III

THE DRAGON RISES

LI

'Twas silent on the astral plane
as dusk did fall, and silhouette
the mountains and the falling rain
did lend an air of sorrow. Yet,
a light sprang up within the dragon's lair.
The headless body lay quite still –
completely motionless it was.
And Attie had been sure the kill
was consummate, and this because
all seven heads she had remov-ed there.

LII

The light, it seemed to emanate
from dragon's body, scaly green.
And thus did now accumulate
around the place the heads had been.
And flesh did there begin to form anew.
First, seven skulls of darkest bone
now formed themselves about the necks
and then it seemed as if a loam
the dragon skulls did then bedeck
solidifying right before our view.

LIII

With flesh full formed, the dragon stirred
– a reflex motion in its wing.
Then faintest noise, it could be heard
and in the throats there did begin
a sound familiar to the astral plane.
The dragon moved and rais-ed up
its scaly muscles, twitching now
and from the air it sought to sup
and sucking breath it did allow
the scream of dragonsong to sound again.

LIV

The song did emanate abroad
and all did know full well, and fear
the terrifying sound they heard
was dragonsong, and were full clear
it meant that Harmony was living once again.
And all did hide them in that place
for none could counter dragonsong
and all did fear to see the face
of dragon –all but Oberon
who calmly thus now waited for her there.

LV

'Twas three years since the Seer left
to seek his lover, Harmony
and Albion was then bereft
of second sight and power to see
the plans the elfin army did employ.
Thus, Oberon did penetrate
deep into land of Albion
and greatly did he desecrate
the sacred places, and had gone
to length unknown, the humans to destroy.

LVI

But Oberon was in a rage
for fact that Merlin still did strive
and greater magic did engage
than he himself could thus derive
as he his evil purpose did pursue.
But if by use of subterfuge
he could the dragon now employ
with all the hate she did exude,
he Merlin's might could yet destroy
and overrun the human land anew.

LVII

So thus he waited in that place
as she did maddened pain excise
then placed himself before her face,
for still she did not realise
that he was architect of all her ill.
Then spake he up in confidence,
"Hail, Harmony, thou Queen of Death.
Now, wouldst thou seek some recompense
for reason that thy lover's breath
was ripped from him by virtue of the will..."

LVIII

"...of thy dear Father, Merlin – see
the love that he holds unto you
and know that only canst thou be
at rest if thou dost sing anew
thy dragonsong into thy father's face.
And I shall help thee, Harmony,
for none doth care for thee but I
and thou didst service unto me
and thus did clearly justify
my calling thee from Hell's own darkest place."

LIX

The dragon looked upon the elf
and just enough humanity
did she possess within herself
to know that what he said to be
the case was true. And so she thus did owe
a debt unto her father now
that surely soon must be repaid.
Thus unto Albion she'd go
with Merlin, now to seek a trade:
his blood for Vidar's blood would surely flow.

LX

Thus dragon rose into the sky
and lit the darkness with her flame
and through the heavens she did fly
and unto Albion came again,
there to confront with Merlin at the last.
And Merlin, deep within his mind
did clearly see what came to be
but energy he could not find
to show his daughter, Harmony,
the evil lie, the elf, for truth, had passed.

LXI

And thus, unto the astral plane
did Merlin come with full intent
to speak with Harmony again
and of this task would not repent,
but came in time to watch her fly away.
And as he stood in weakened state
did Oberon come unto him
and hailed him: "Merlin, yet too late
art thou to stop the dragon-sin!
She heads for Albion to repay…"

LXII

"…thee for thy love and deepest care
by burning now Arthurian Court.
And so it is that 'Bekah fair
who at thy hand was magic taught,
will use her evil powers for darkest ends.
She will thy kingdom now destroy
that thou hast judged for centuries
and darkest magic will employ
and nothing now will her appease.
I tried to stop her, Merlin – we are friends!"

LXIII

"Thou know'st the care I have for thee –
how I revere thy wisdom, and
thy values have I sought to see
as I have judged the elfin land –
my deep respect is evidenced to thee!"
Thus did the elf the wizard mock
as Merlin faced his darkest hour.
He hoped his confidence to rock
and his devotion to devour
and to destroy him now, through Harmony.

LXIV

But Merlin slowly turned to him
and looked into his elfin eyes.
He saw the blackness deep within
and how all truth he did despise
and knew he then the darkness of his soul.
And thus it was quite evident
that Gaia never would be free –
for Oberon would not relent
'till he destroyed humanity.
For Gaia's subjugation was his goal.

LXV

Then lifted Merlin up his voice
and spoke to Oberon anew.
"My son, I think thou once had choice
and could keep truth within thy view.
But now I do perceive no choice at all.
The evil that thou dost pursue
hath ripped thy heart from out thy breast.
And all that's good and all that's true
has left thee long, and full bereft
art thou, and this will surely cause thy fall."

LXVI

"Indefinitely, nothing lasts,
But all doth end in its due time.
And fate doth see thee as it casts
the dice once more, and full sublime
thine end shall be, when now thy time doth come.
Mine own time here, it is now short
and there is nothing thou canst do
to hurt me, for my heart is taught
that evil thou wilt ever do.
Beware! Thy final act –it hath begun."

LXVII

"So I shall leave thee to thy fate.
I need no magic thee to quell
or lightning bolt to demonstrate,
or potions, chants, or even spell.
For God's own truth will evil overcome."
And with these words he turned around
and slowly, then, he walked away.
But Oberon would stand his ground
and sought some clever word to say.
But now within his heart he could find none.

LXVIII

Then Merlin would to Albion
return for he did clearly see
he had to end the dragonsong,
and thus must speak with Harmony
and ready her for Sleep Stone that would come
at Seer's hands and Attie too,
who even now the wastes did brave.
And when they came it would be true
that they all Gaia would now save.
And then at last would all their work be done.

LXIX

But Oberon enrag-ed was
that Merlin did speak thus to him.
He flew to Elfindom because
potential for yet greater sin
did he perceive present itself that day.
And subterfuge he did employ
and magic black now to procure
the knowledge needed to destroy
the purposes of good, for sure.
Thus, knowledge of the Sleep Stone came his way.

LXX

For gazed he in his Pool of Sight.
And there did Lady Attie see,
and Seer Michael at her right
hand, as they now did constantly
the Stone of Sleep pursue in Elfindom.
And it was unto him revealed
the demon army would thus wake
if e'er the Gate could be unsealed,
if any man the Stone did take
for more than single cycle of the sun.

LXXI

Thus once again to witchcraft turned
the evil elf and call-ed to
the King of Demons as he yearned
for greater pow'r and strength anew
and with the Dark One, evil bargain sought.
Then once again the Demon King
did rise to Gaia and did make
an opportunity for sin.
Again did Oberon forsake
all thought of righteousness that he was taught.

LXXII

The Dark One stood in front of him.
In dim-lit room his presence came.
No sense of grandeur did begin.
No entourage did there proclaim
him as the darkest, Hellish, evil power.
But how his eyes did penetrate
deep into Oberon's very soul
and satisfied as to his state –
the elf could never be made whole –
he bargain struck with him that very hour.

LXXIII

"Now, Oberon," the Dark One said,
"what dost thou seek from Hell today?
And where will now thy soul be led?
And what will be thy choice of way?
And what is it thou off'rest for thy fate?"
"My offer is straightforward now,"
replied then Oberon to him.
"My immortality allow,
and surely now I shall begin
removal of the Sleep Stone from the Gate."

LXXIV

"The humans do pursue the Stone,
and seek to make the dragon sleep,
intending that it should be gone
but briefly, and would surely keep
the demon army safe within the Gate.
But if my elfin army moves,
preventing them returning it,
and opportunity now proves
to free thy demons from the pit
wherein they sleep, and thus a different fate…"

LXXV

"...doth fall to Gaia and to me
then both shall be compatible.
For I would now thy vassal be
and rule all Gaia as thy tool.
Then demon power shall all the world o'rtake!"
The Demon King stood deep in thought
and weighed he there most carefully
this plan that was with dangers fraught.
For he was bound eternally
his deepest bargain never to forsake.

LXXVI

But bargain made from dawn of time
did no longer ambition suit
and thought he, Gaia shall be mine!
And greater power shall be the fruit
of breaking now, my bargain bound in fate.
And if by happenstance it falls
this plan shall fail and be destroyed,
and any then unto me calls
that I account for means employed
of freeing demons from within the Gate...

LXXVII

…then I shall merely blame this fool
and end his immortality.
For thus, he shall be just my tool
and all will ever plainly see
that he for all this is full culpable.
So he to Oberon replied
"It surely is as thou dost state.
But know thou this: if thou has lied,
eternal pain shall be thy fate.
Eternal life I'll not give to a fool."

LXXVIII

"For I shall grant here unto thee
eternal life thou dost desire
if thou my honest servant be
and in my service do not tire.
Thus, unto thee I shall now prophesy:
no natur'l death shall be thy fate.
No man shall kill thee by the sword.
No accident shall terminate
thy endless life – so be this heard!
Be servant of the Dark One – never die!"

LXXIX

Thus Oberon possessed now was
with thoughts of power and endless days.
For nothing else he cared, because
he evil made in all his ways.
And so the bargain then in blood was made.
Thus he returned to elfin Lords
and not a word to them did speak
that he was free of mortal chords
and for eternity would seek
to rule the whole of Gaia by this trade.

IV

THE GUARDIANS OF THE STONE

LXXX

When Attie and the Seer left
the little cabin by the lake
she thought herself now full bereft
and surely that her heart would break
For Michael loved the dragon and not her.
But here was chance for her to prove
her love and benefit to him.
And seeing this, perhaps he'd love
her as he tried now to begin
to see the truth of dragon and concur…

LXXXI

…that Harmony did never care
or ever really love him true.
She thought by being with him there
now to her credit would accrue
her honesty and selflessness that day.
For she her interests laid aside
when now, together, did they seek
the Sleeping Stone and must decide
together how they meant to keep
the Lord of Fire and Lord of Ice at bay.

LXXXII

But now she set aside such thought
and on the task did concentrate.
She knew the journey would be fraught,
and dangerous to penetrate
was Elfindom, with kingdoms all at war.
So thus they travelled in the night
and in the day did take their sleep
and so avoided Elfish might
and to themselves now did they keep.
And thus did little time now pass before…

LXXXIII

…they stood within the frozen hills
in northern parts of Elfindom.
Yet strangely both did feel their wills
diminished now from going on,
till Michael suddenly the cause did face.
"'Tis magic, Attie, we confront!
A spell is cast within this place.
And those that come here bear the brunt
of such, and their depression face.
'Tis this that ever keeps the Stone in place."

LXXXIV

"Then let us rise, My Love," said she,
"and stand against our feelings now.
For standing close together, we
support each other and allow
no space for darkness to frustrate our cause.
We two the Sleep Stone must retrieve.
And even if it costs me dear
this gift I shall to Gaia give.
My duty now to me is clear.
In reaching this objective I'll not pause."

LXXXV

Then wrapped they cloaks about themselves
and set their face to sleet and snow.
And keeping watchful eyes for elves,
into the mountains they did go.
They tried the best they could to motivate
themselves against depression now
that ever would envelop them.
They knew they must not simply bow
to darkness that would enter in
their hearts and thus their purpose denigrate.

LXXXVI

But each day as they deeper came
into the frozen mountain range
did Attie, who was much the same,
in Michael start to see a change.
And he did now withdraw within his mind,
as they did ever onward go
for cause that he did sense the Stone.
And this, his inner sight did show.
Thus he did know that he alone
must face the Guardians, and must leave behind…

LXXXVII

…the Lady Attie, who would wait
as he did enter deep within
the mountainside, to seek the Gate
to Hell. And thus, he would begin
to take the Sleep Stone that would lay to rest
his Love, who had great evil done –
but greater yet had been deceived.
And Michael knew he must atone
or Gaia would not be relieved
though he, of love, he knew was now bereft.

LXXXVIII

So when they came unto a cave,
with gentleness he turned unto
the Lady, who would him now save
and spare deep pain that would accrue
to him when he did venture on alone.
But looked he gently in her eyes
and raised his hand to touch her cheek
so that she then did realise
the Seer was not truly weak
but inner strength possessed he of his own.

LXXXIX

"My dearest Attie," spake he then,
"thou knowest what I say to thee.
That I cannot e'en now begin
to show thee what inside I see.
But I must enter in the mountainside.
For where I go thou canst not come.
It is my part to face alone
the Guardians. I now become
the sole pursuer of the Stone
whilst thou at mouth of cave must now abide."

XC

"For days I have now been aware
the Lord of Fire and Lord of Ice
are mine alone –I am full clear
they'll take no other sacrifice.
And I the dragon must now lay to rest.
For by my sin I know I caused
the wrath of dragonsong to sound.
For if I had not with her paused
on astral plane, but gone to ground
of Albion, and given of my best…"

XCI

"…in Arthur's cause and set myself
to duties there in Albion,
she would have turned unto the elf
and maybe back to Hell be gone.
Thus, for this I know I am culpable.
And thus it falls to me alone
to stand before the Guardians
and by this act may I atone
for all the wrong that I have done.
For I alone am now accountable."

XCII

As Attie listened to his speech
the tears did trickle down her face.
She knew that she could not him reach
and he must enter in that place
confronting Lords of Fire and Ice alone.
She had no words to comfort him
but simply took him by the hand;
and looked into his soul within;
and told him she did understand
his need within himself now to atone.

XCIII

"I love thee, Michael," whispered she,
and looking deep within his eyes,
knew what he spake would have to be
and fully did she realise
the depth of torment that was in his soul.
She knew that he confronted thus
the Guardians who held the Stone.
And though the chance was tenuous
'Twas one he had to take alone
or never, ever would he be made whole.

XCIV

Then not another word was spoke
as Michael turned away from her.
And this choice would he not revoke
nor unto any would defer.
Thus, Michael stepped into the mountainside.
And in the dark he lit a light
and knew that he must venture deep.
Within this place no human might
from danger could his life now keep.
Nor was there any single place to hide.

XCV

And thus it was he did descend
into the bowels of the land
and entered places far beyond
the reach of any helping hand
and there would now confront his deepest fears.
The darkness held great terror now
as there himself he did confront.
And knew he that he must, somehow,
his very inner demons hunt
— those that had slept inside him through the years.

XCVI

For these were every bit as real,
as now the darkness did descend,
as those that soon he must reveal
when he the Stone did apprehend,
and take it as a prize to Albion.
And in his soul his demons screamed
and all the pain of childhood years,
and all the love of which he dreamed,
and all the terrors that he feared
confronted him as he did walk alone.

XCVII

And yet he ventured ever on
descending deep into the soil
and unto Guardians soon would come
and would not from this task recoil.
So thus it was he came unto the Gate.
And there, as Merlin prophesied
the Lord of Ice and Lord of Fire
did stand before him, side by side
and never, ever did they tire.
Thus wondered Michael, what would be his fate.

XCVIII

The Guardi'ns spake in unison,
"Frail human, why dost thou come here?
Why hast thou unto Hell's Gate come?
Art thou a fool to have no fear?
For from this place no man has made return."
But Michael spake in confidence,
"Thou knowest why I stand alone
before thee –that this represents
a plea that thou wouldst free the Stone.
For silence from the dragonsong I yearn."

XCIX

"Thou speakest well, thou human man
and doth not fear thy cause to state.
Then know this now: since time began
the Guardians have held this Gate
and to the Gate, the Stone, it is the key.
Thou knowest if the Stone be gone
the demon army will awake
within one cycle of the sun
and they would surely perpetrate
such evil as did Gaia never see."

C

"And if we give to thee the Stone
how can we know thou wilt return
and we will not then face alone
the demon army that doth yearn
for wakefulness and freedom from this place?"
Quoth Michael, "It is obvious
that you have held since time began
your duty on behalf of us
— the gods, the elves and also man.
Now weariness I see upon your face."

CI

"And thus I shall now undertake
to get me back unto this place
and when I come here I shall make
thy task, my task, and thus shall face
eternity here where my Love will sleep.
And thou may both then take some rest
and I shall stand before the Gate.
For I by death have been caressed
and for me now it is too late
for peace, and I no company do keep."

CII

The Guardians then did confer
between them and did this accept:
that they to Seer would defer
for what he said was full correct.
The Guardians felt they had stood too long.
And giving unto him the Stone
gave them the chance to be set free.
If Michael would then stand alone
and hold the Gate then he would see
his land and world set free from dragonsong.

CIII

Thus freely did they give to him
the Amulet, the Stone of Sleep
and quickly now did he begin
the journey back and way to seek.
For he did have one cycle of the sun,
the task to fill and to return
the Stone unto appointed place.
Then greatly did the Seer yearn
his former steps now to retrace
and wished his final work was now begun.

CIV

He climbed up through the mountainside
till light of sun did touch his face
and there saw Attie, who did bide
her time and waited in that place
in patience for the Seer to return.
And when she saw him thus emerge
from darkest cave, and clutching Stone,
within her, then her heart did surge
and wished she that they could be gone
so deeply for his love she did now yearn.

CV

"Come, Attie," quoth the Seer then.
"There is no time to lose, for we
have but one cycle of the sun
before the Stone replaced must be –
or shall the demon army then awake.
So let us rise to astral plane
and travel unto Freedom now,
where surely Merlin comes again
and brings the dragon there somehow.
The Stone the power of evil shall now break."

CVI

Then took he Attie by the hand
and rose they thence to astral plane,
and they did fly across the land
and unto Freedom came again
as sun did rise inexorably high'r.
And thus, they waited by the lake
for Merlin to come to that place
and fervently for Gaia's sake
did wish that he would speed his pace,
and knew they not how deep his soul did tire.

V

DRAGON LOVE

CVII

The dragon came to Albion
as morning light did touch the land
and not a sound of dragonsong
escaped her lips as she did stand
upon the soil of Gaia once again.
She stood before Arthurian Court.
The light did her illuminate.
And for her father now she sought
and on this thought did ruminate:
that he his final lesson must be taught.

CVIII

The sun, it rose into the sky
and mused she that, upon this day
she would her father make comply,
and maybe this would take away
the depths of torment that her heart did feel.
For mostly now, and oftentime,
of sanity was she bereft.
Her human thought, it did decline,
and mostly dragon heart was left.
And Merlin's death that process might now seal.

CIX

As sun did make the shadows long
did Harmony a mighty roar
exude, and thus did dragonsong
resound within the land once more,
and mothers held their children to their breasts.
And those that then did walk abroad
fled to their homes at rapid pace.
And those who had, did take their swords
and hid themselves in safest place,
and put their breastplates close upon their chests.

CX

For all did know the fearful sound
and all were truly terrified.
The dragonsong did now resound
and once again it did abide
in Gaia –and still worse, in Albion.
Then roar-ed Harmony in rage,
"Show me my father, bring him here!
For nothing will my hate assuage
until I see him kneel in fear
and shed his blood for Vidar, who is gone."

CXI

But nothing did disturb the sound
of wind that blew between the trees.
No battle cry did there resound
No army came now, her to seize.
Only before her rose the blinding sun.
Then with no warning, nor with sound,
did Merlin stand before the Court
and thus did occupy the ground,
the very place that she had sought
to tear him bodily, as had been done...

CXII

...to Vidar, many decades past
as she now never could forget.
Her memory would ever last
and in her heart was fully set –
however much the dragon nature raged.
Then Merlin gently lifted up
his voice and to his daughter spake,
"My love-child, thou didst surely sup
a bitter drink –thy heart did break
and ever in this pain it is engaged."

CXIII

"Canst thou hear me, my precious child?
Or is thy mind deluded so?
And is thy nature now too wild
to take on human form and go
and walk with me and talk with me this day?"
The dragon stood its ground, but thought.
And deep within a tiny sound –
a single word it had been taught
replete with meaning, full profound:
'Twas 'righteousness' – a word she could not say.

CXIV

Her voice did growl from deep within,
"Why hast thou been the cause of death?
And was my lover lost in sin
that thou should leave me thus bereft
and aching, now, into death's arms to fly?
And for thee now, no love I have
but hold thee just in deep contempt.
But unto thee my gift I'd give
and then my anger would be spent.
My father: 'tis a perfect day to die."

CXV

He would have told her of his love;
he would have held her close and cried;
he would have raised her high above
her pain, he surely would have tried
his dearest child to keep still by his side.
But he could not reach unto her
for she was wracked with pain inside,
and to his love would not defer
and pain with love – it surely vied.
But pain did win, and she did thus abide...

CXVI

...in dragon form with twisted mind
and thus did rock herself in pain.
And torment her did once more find
and madness came to her again
as from her lips did single sound escape.
"Die" was the only word she spoke
and Merlin answered not a word
nor would his love for her revoke
nor would the truth be ever heard
by her from him as she did seal his fate.

CXVII

He looked deep into dragon eyes
and sought for sign of 'Bekah fair.
Her suffering did not despise –
but he could see no human there,
and thus he did accept he'd pay the price.
Though he no evil now had done,
and righteousness, it was his part
unto his limit he had come
and utterly she broke his heart.
So he would make the final sacrifice.

CXVIII

But as she stood, she seemed to doubt
and indecision tore her heart.
Perhaps she would have turned about
and maybe sought a better part –
till Oberon appeared before them both.
He looked into the dragon's face
and needed not a word to speak.
His presence now within that place
reminded her that she did seek
full recompense, and thus it was she quoth…

CXIX

…"It shall be done." No other word
as she to Merlin then did turn.
And from him not a sound was heard
as dragon breath did greatly burn
his body and did char him in a flash.
And as his frame, it there did fall
did Oberon scream in delight –
for he was architect of all
and revelled now that dragon might
had turned his adversary unto ash.

CXX

The dragon stood then motionless
and contemplated what she'd done
to him who did her oft caress
and who her life had once begun.
No sense of satisfaction did she get.
Then Oberon remov-ed hence
to elfin camp, his troops to move.
And with them now would make defence
of elfin mountains, now to prove
the power of evil e'er the sun did set.

CXXI

Then all the Elfish troops he took
by pow'r of magic from that place
and when the humans then did look
no sign of elves now could they trace.
Then thought they Albion was free at last
from Elfish threat unto their peace.
And there they great rejoicing made
and thought that they had found release,
and Elfish threat they did evade.
But Harmony did stand in pain, aghast.

CXXII

For yet more torment did she feel
as sin to sin, it did give way.
And nothing deep inside would heal
nor even did her spirits say
that she her final torment did now seal.
For now her love of life was dead
and desperately did she wish
to end her being, and be led
to place where she, though dragonish,
some sense of her humanity could feel.

CXXIII

And far away from Albion
beside the cabin by the lake
did Michael see all that was done
and shook he, as his heart did break
to see his lover now his father kill.
He wept profusely as he knelt
that surely all would now be lost
and wracked was he with deepest guilt
and ever would he count the cost.
And deeply of this pain he drank his fill.

CXXIV

Then took he Attie by the hand
and led her thence by magic power
and them removed to Albion's land
and stood they then that very hour
before the dragon, who spake not to Seer.
Thus, silent looked he on her now
and not a word his heart could speak
and surely wished that he somehow
could time reverse, and he did seek
to Harmony the truth now to make clear.

CXXV

The shadows lengthened in that place.
The sands of time inex'rably
within the glass did surely race.
And Attie thought that it must be
too late to put the Stone back in its place.
But Michael stood in confidence
before the dragon and thus quoth,
"My dearest love, dost thou now sense
that thou and I once took an oath
to love eternally, and thus to face…"

CXXVI

"…the future, calmly, hand-in-hand
and of that love I will now speak
as now I do before thee stand
and thy humanity do seek.
Wilt thou thy human form now take again?
For I would merely walk with thee
a while, and seek thee to remind,
and put before thy face to see
some memories of humankind
of time when we did love. And surely then…"

CXXVII

"…thou wilt recall I loved thee so.
And ever, ever shall I love.
And unto depths of Hell would go
if by so doing, thou'd approve
of me, and my love then reciprocate.
For I am sure thou loved me true.
But thou didst think that for thy lie
that I would keep within my view
dishonesty – that thou didst try
to keep from me thy dragon form and fate."

CXXVIII

"It would have mattered not to me
that thou didst once conceal the truth.
The things I loved in thee to see
were true about thee from thy youth
and I would not eschew thy darker side.
So why didst thou choose me to blind
and send me far away from thee?
For though this time is far behind
forever is thy love to me
revealed, and doth within me now abide."

CXXIX

And as the Seer poured his heart
before the dragon in that place
did Harmony now make a start
to change, and stood before his face
her human form that Michael had loved so.
And there she fell upon her knees
and wept and wept her heart away
and thought she that she now might seize
one final chance, and to him say
that him, she loved, before to Hell she'd go.

CXXX

But as she came to human form
he threw his arms about her frame
and rivers of his tears did come
and wept he, until Attie came
and gently there did separate the two.
"There's work to do," she softly said,
"and time, it is our enemy.
For deeply now it is my dread
that we shall past the limit be
and Gaia shall be terrorised anew."

CXXXI

Then Michael knew within his heart
that Harmony would surely come,
and with him now would make a start.
Then they would end the work begun,
and let the dragon sleep before the Gate.
And so they rose to fly from there
by power of Michael's magic now
and surely nothing did compare
with deepest pain that he somehow
did have to bear, in leading Harmony unto her fate.

VI
THE FINAL CONFLICT

CXXXII

Thus Michael carried Harmony
as even then the sun did fall,
and Attie then could clearly see
that unto them the Gate did call
to place the Sleep Stone back within the day.
But when they came unto the cave
they saw the Elfish army there
which even now they sought to brave
and for their lives held not a care
but knew that Oberon would bar the way.

CXXXIII

And there they thus, exhausted, fell
and knew not whence their help would come.
For if they barred not gate to Hell
before the rising of the sun
the demon army would be fully woke.
And they the world would overrun
and human life would be erased
and then from pow'r of Oberon
would nothing ever now be saved
and no man could this principle revoke.

CXXXIV

Then Michael gently laid to rest
the sleeping form of Harmony
and felt at last this final test
required of him that he should be
much greater than the strength that he possessed.
And thus he looked in Attie's eyes,
and weariness of soul did see
and once again did realise
the warmth he held for her, as she
seemed now, as he, of energy bereft.

CXXXV

"What shall we do, my love?" she asked,
as sat they quietly in the dark.
"Impossibly we are now tasked
though thought we once to make our mark
on Gaia for the sake of dearest good.
Is all our work in vain?" she said.
"I cannot see how this can be.
For while I live and am not dead,
then I shall thus refuse to see
the power of evil win, and thus I should..."

CXXXVI

"...a way of overcoming find.
But I exhausted am, and now
tormented deep within my mind
to find another way somehow
to place the Sleep Stone back within the Gate."
And thus it was, exhausted, they
did lay them down and fall asleep
despite the fact that soon the day
would break, and open fissure deep,
into the mountain and the demons wake.

CXXXVII

But in the night did come a dream
unto the Seer as he lay.
And it did then unto him seem
that Merlin did pass by that way
and walked with him, and talked with him a spell.
"My son," said Merlin unto him,
"why dost thou sleep with work to do?
For thou should surely now begin
to call to gods of Asgard, who
alone this power of evil can now quell."

CXXXVIII

Then all at once did Michael know
exactly what he had to do.
He quickly woke and made a show
to waken Attie, for she too
a crucial part in outcome would now play.
"Now gird thyself, thou warrior!"
he called to her, in strength anew.
"For we shall not to sin defer
but keeping righteousness in view,
shall yet replace the Stone within this day!"

CXXXIX

Thus, Attie readied then herself
for conflict, and put on her sword.
And clearly knew she, that the elf
would soon confront her, and the word
the King of Demons spoke would now come true.
Then, as the dawn was set to break
did Michael enter into trance
and unto Asgard him did take
to offer there this circumstance:
that Gaia was in need of godly hue.

CXL

Now in the elfin camp, as dawn
was surely then about to break,
were elfin Lords then fully torn
and wished they to their king forsake,
but would not, for the terrors that he held.
But Oberon was now aroused –
excitement brewed within his heart.
For evil had he long espoused,
and thus, it soon would make a start
to conquer all as demon power unfurled.

CXLI

But up in Asgard, Michael made
a case for intervention now,
by gods, who thus were sore afraid
the Demon King would break his vow
– the bargain of eternity he broke.
And thus it was the gods did come
to Gaia as the day did break.
For Odin, thus with Thor, his son,
and Nanna did the heavens shake.
The power of Demon King they would revoke.

CXLII

Thus, as the sun did start to rise,
and demons stirred within the hill,
did Thor and Odin realise
that time would have to be made still.
And Nanna held, within its course, the moon,
while Thor and Odin held the sun
and time stood still within that place.
And demon work, though once begun,
they very soon would now erase.
And Attie called to combat Oberon!

CXLIII

She stood upon the mountainside
with brown hair blowing in the wind
and sword in scabbard by her side
and thus was fully disciplined
to meet the evil elf a final time.
"Come forth, thou source of evilness!
And meet me now in combat here!
And then my sword shall thee caress
unless, of course, thou dost hold fear.
I tell thee that this day thy life is mine!"

CXLIV

But Ob'ron laughed himself in mirth.
For he did hold mortality
in deep contempt, of little worth
was Attie's challenge, but thought he
a chance it gave to show his Lords his power.
And so he rose up in the camp,
and out to Attie then strode he;
was confident that daylight's lamp
did mark the new dawn he would see
when demon life did now begin to flower.

CXLV

They stood one hundred yards apart.
He looked on her with deep contempt.
Then gazed she back with steadfast heart
and knew her task was heaven-sent
and that the gods were with her on that day.
And only as the daylight broke
did Oberon begin to ask
if Demon King might now revoke
permitting deadline now to pass.
For demons did not walk within that way.

CXLVI

As Attie thus advanced on him
at last did he begin to doubt
the Demon's promise, and begin
to wonder if he stood without
the power of immortality that day.
His magic now deserted him
as at him, inexorably
did Attie come, and did begin
the terror in his eyes to see
that possibly his life she'd take away.

CXLVII

"Dost thou have anything to say?"
she asked him as she drew her sword.
But fear did keep his voice at bay
and spoke he to her not a word
as she did stand before him, full of power.
She lifted up her sword on high
and then she brought it crashing in
upon the elf who did rely
on promise of the Demon King –
whose full veracity he saw that hour.

CXLVIII

For thus, no accident befell
him as he dropped where he did stand
and by no man was sent to hell
but rather by a woman's hand
was demon prophecy now deep fulfilled.
And Elfish Lords did stand aghast
as Oberon did die that day.
But knew they freedom now at last
and could return unto the way
of peace, and thus might Elfindom be healed.

VII

EVENTIDE

CXLIX

Then Michael, now return-ed there,
did come to Attie, and thus spoke,
"We must get hence, for I do fear
the gods will not for long revoke
the passage of the sun within the day."
So Attie lifted up the Stone
and Michael carried Harmony.
And very soon they were now gone
unto the cave where she did see
that once again, he must, within his way...

CL

...descend into the earth alone.
To meet the Lords of Fire and Ice
with Harmony he did now come,
and he did mean to sacrifice
himself and take his place within the Gate.
This he had promised hours before,
so that the Lords might be set free.
And then fulfilled would be the Law,
and he would be with Harmony.
For thus, together, would he set their fate.

CLI

But as he travelled deep within
the earth, did Harmony awake.
And thus she did speak unto him
and sought that he would promise make:
to let another woman love him now.
And in the dark he held her tight
as stood they there before the Gate.
And tried he then with all his might
his other life now to forsake
– to stay with her and never, ever let her go.

CLII

But gently did she from him take
the Stone of Sleep, the Amulet.
And thought he now his heart would break
as she around her neck did set
the Stone, and sadly there before him lay.
He knelt with her as then she lay.
He in the dark did feel her gaze
and deeply sought he to defray
and final price now to erase.
Then kissed he her one final time that day.

CLIII

The Lords of Fire and Ice did sleep
as Harmony between them lay
and Sleeping Stone did demons keep
full safe within the Gate that day.
Then Michael slowly turned around and left.
Then climbed he through the mountainside
and wept his heart out as he climbed.
And tears would he now not deride,
for love he had left far behind
and of his dearest lover was bereft.

CLIV

His heart did shriek within him now
as he did climb towards the light.
His passion lay there, far below
and all his strength had taken flight.
For desperately sought he love to keep.
But mind is such powerful tool
and as he climbed he did forget.
Then knew he that his heart would cool
and wanted he now to be left,
to sleep; to sleep; to sleep; to sleep; to sleep.

CLV

As he emerged now from the cave
did Attie stand in front of him
and sought again his pain to save
and wished to show him love again.
But empty was his heart, and it did bleed.
And as these two conversed that day
the Spirit of the Wizard came
and walk-ed with them in the way.
And thus did Merlin once again
advise these two on how they should proceed.

CLVI

"Dear Attie," said he unto her,
"thy future lies in Freedom's land.
And in this, Judges do concur
that thou must take a Judgeship, and
great wisdom shall thou lend when thou dost come.
But I cannot stand in the way
of Oberon's deep prophecy.
This is the price that thou must pay
and thus thy future spent will be,
alone; alone; alone; alone; alone."

CLVII

Then Attie fell upon her knees
and wept for knowledge of this truth.
And though his words did not her please,
this had she known since early youth
that she alone was destined thus to be.
Then Merlin unto Michael turned
and smiled upon his dearest son.
"My son, thou hast for death long yearned
and long wished life had not begun.
But this is not the future thou wilt see."

CLVIII

"For Albion calls unto thee.
A Judgeship thou must also take.
For though thou view death preferably,
thy duty must thou not forsake,
and thou must also dwell on Gaia alone."
Then Michael lifted up his heart
and wept to moon and stars and sun
and in frustration made a start
to end this story now begun
and cried, "Atone! Atone! Atone! Atone!"

CLIX

And thus it is we leave this place.
Three figures on the mountainside:
their history we did full trace,
and how their sadness doth abide!
For I do merely tell what I do see.
So have I now an ending made
acceptable to gods and man?
Or wilt thou, reader, now persuade
me once again to take my pen
and make another story come to be?

ACKNOWLEDGEMENTS

I would like to thank Sandra Boyes, Dani Witkowski and my daughters Naomi Jacobs and Vici Derrett for their reading of and comments on early drafts of the text.

Similar thanks go to Jacqueline Haskell, and Sue Aldworth for their reading of and comments on the later drafts.

Finally, I must acknowledge the huge contribution of Dr Stephen Carver of Green Door Design (www.greendoordp.com) for helping me to understand the historical heritage of the work and instilling sufficient confidence in me to publish it.

ABOUT THE AUTHOR

Some are born with silver spoons in their mouths. Michael Forester was born with a pen in his hand. His first published creative work, *If It Wasn't For That Dog*, was about his first year with his beloved hearing dog, Matt.

He is a Winchester Writers' Festival prize-winner and has been long/shortlisted three times in the Fish Writing Contest.

His first novel, *Vicious* (a story of punk rock, the second coming of the Messiah and the true nature of the universe), was showcased by The Literary Consultancy in November 2015.

Michael's children look on aghast as he squanders their inheritance on such profligacies as A4 printing paper. They need have no concern. He plans to leave them the pen.

OTHER BOOKS BY MICHAEL FORESTER

PREVIOUSLY BY THE AUTHOR:

If It Wasn't For That Dog

FORTHCOMING:

Vicious

Daughter of Man

For more information see Michael Forester's web site:

www.michaelforester.co.uk